Endée Quaï Press

ADAM DREAMT

Nicholas Kyriacos lives and works in Sydney

ALSO BY NICHOLAS KYRIACOS

Billy's Tree

*The Fall of Donnald Trummp,
Sarrah Pallin, Hillary Clinnton, Anon 1488 ...
and The Rise of The Coyote!*

ADAM DREAMT

NICHOLAS KYRIACOS

Published in Australia in 2023 by Endée Quaï Press
ABN: 2157 8447153
endeequai@gmail.com
nicholaskyriacos.com.au

A catalogue record for this work is available from the
National Library of Australia

ISBN: 978-0-6456665-5-7 (Paperback)
ISBN: 978-0-6456665-6-4 (Ebook)

Edited by Peter Vaughan-Reid
Typeset in Calluna 10.5/15pt by Seymour Design
Printed by IngramSpark Australia

In memoriam: George Orwell

As he stood waiting for the flesh to be loosened on him, he prayed for greater clarity, and it became as obvious as a hand. It was clear that One, and no other figure, is the answer to all sums.

PATRICK WHITE

Prologue

On the morning the Queen of AntLand was going to deliver her historical address to her subjects, Adam Ant, The Royal Forager and Grand Protector of Food Supplies, awoke feeling an acute sense of anxiety. It should have been a day of celebration for Adam, as it was for the other thirty million or so citizens of the empire, but something, Adam knew, was amiss with AntLand. What it was he could not quite put his claw on.

Adam Ant, recently appointed by Her Majesty to The Council of Elders, was to know, by the time night had fallen on this unprecedented day, that his life and that of AntLand would never be the same.

Chapter 1

Genesis

In The Holy AntBook it is written that 388 months prior to delivering her historical address to her assembled subjects, Queen Ant unfurled her pliable, transparent wings and took to the air, flying alone from the land of her birth to the centre of The Eternal Valley. From the air, she gazed in every direction with her huge, infrared eyes, her antennae, set wide apart on her broad head, trembling in anticipation. It is written that upon landing she savoured the soil, after which she looked in wonder at the vast, fertile plains stretching to the base of the monumental snow-topped Sacred Circle of Cliffs that formed what the Queen knew to be a gift bestowed on her and her future subjects: an impenetrable barrier to what some came to know as The Great Darkness and others referred to as The NoWorld. She had, she knew, been guided to this part of the valley by AntGod's unseen mandible. It had been intended, and so it was good.

It is written that moments after Queen Ant alighted on The Eternal Valley, she contorted her middle legs, bore down onto her wings then snapped them off. She offered a prayer to AntGod, emitting pheromones from her abdomen, her head and legs, holding aloft her great mandibles in supplication, obedience and thankfulness. She paused, despite the danger presented by predators, knowing that once she departed this basin and entered her subterranean world to begin the creation of a mighty metropolis, she would never again see the surface of her world, would never again rest her eyes on the flat, rich plains or the comforting shadows cast by those imposing mountainous cliffs. The holy grains of soil upon which she landed would, she immediately decided, be collected ceremonially by the first of her offspring. With the dignity such a ritual demanded, they would then be secreted in a location known only to herself and those she would appoint as her governing Elders, to be displayed and perhaps paraded on some future occasion that warranted such an honour.

The ground was damp but not wet. It was soft, too, another blessing, and so Queen Ant was able to make quick progress, digging a perpendicular tunnel three times the length of her body in one day. It took her five days to dig out a large opening, which she named The Imperial Gate, and a chamber in which she laid her first eggs. When the eggs hatched into larvae, she fed them fat stored in her body. Once reared, some of these ants took to foraging, returning with the carcasses of spiders, flies and mosquitoes. A dozen or so spent their days dampening and cuddling her while others assisted her in enlarging the nest. It took a further sixty-five days to excavate a tunnel exactly 400 times her body length. The following eight days were devoted to the creation of The Royal Chamber in which it had been intended she would seal herself forever, seeing out her life laying eggs.

In the 388 months since the empire's founding, her highness had given birth to over a quarter of a billion black offspring. So it is written; so it has been done.

And now, for the first time since she had been led to her hallowed land and hidden herself from the sun and the eyes of her subjects – except, of course, from those who had been chosen to care for her personal needs, transport her eggs to the nursery and, like Adam, serve on her Council of Elders – for the first time since she had devoted herself without question to AntGod's will, she was to emerge from The Royal Chamber and address her subjects. This was unprecedented. Indeed, some of her subjects were afraid that in going against the natural order of things she might even invite AntGod's retribution.

As The Royal Forager and Grand Protector of Food Supplies, Adam Ant was responsible for more workers than any other member of The Council. And so he was busier than most, guiding his charges into tunnels and rooms into which, when the great moment arrived, specially appointed ants would emit pheromones so that Her Majesty's address was communicated from one subject to the next. Adam instructed his thousands of seed-harvesters to suspend their maintenance of the empire's huge stockpiles to assist his foragers in carrying the honeypot ants into passages wide enough so that their abdomens, swollen like balloons with a rich supply of honey, nectar or dew, were not damaged by the passing traffic of excited ants. These honeypot ants, suspended upside down from the ceiling in a chamber where they expected to see out their entire lives, were overjoyed at being released from their servitude.

Adam scurried through the complex network of passage-ways and arteries, over bridges and through archways, directing his workers to position themselves as close as possible to The Grand Hall, where Her Majesty would be carried to deliver her address. He rushed through the labyrinthine system of tunnels to inspect the larders and to the farms in which their livestock of aphids, caterpillars and greenflies were either milked for their honeydew or bred for their meat and, when satisfied all was in order, dismissed his charges from their labour on this grandest of all grand holy days. He also sent out scouts to ensure that those ants collecting resin above ground – as important as their employment was in preventing infections in the empire – and those gathering food had ceased work and had returned to the metropolis to be present for the history-making occasion.

Close to where the Queen would make her address was Young Nano, a steadfast ant who, despite his youth, had already earned elite status in Adam Ant's eyes by working vigorously at all times and, even more impressively, instigating many chores. Young Nano was known amongst his peers as the ant who could recall routes more accurately than most, using the sun as a lodestar and distinguishing characteristics of the landscape and the ground's odour, which he had memorised on previous hunting excursions. What differentiated him for Adam was his sombre demeanour, his watchful, intelligent eyes and his taut, vigilant antennae: the youngster would observe Adam with an alertness that the Elder found puzzling, flattering and, when the youngster's attention was particularly intense, disconcerting. Adam thought of him with some fondness as The Watching Ant.

When all the AntLanders had taken their position, a great silence and stillness fell on the thousands of tunnels, vaults and chambers in which the Queen's subjects patiently awaited their sovereign's arrival. Those who had been selected to witness the event in The Grand Hall, from where they would be able to gain a glimpse of the Queen herself for the first time in their life, waited with taut apprehension. Some were afraid to lay their eyes upon her and had decided beforehand – lest they be struck down by her magnificence or by the great AntGod Himself for their impudence – to lower their heads in obeisance and look upon the ground in reverence and humility for the entirety of the time it took the Queen to complete her address.

AyJay Heartland, the Queen's Senior Advisor and ChairAnt of The Council of Elders, sent an Imperial Runner to The Royal Chamber to inform the Queen's carers that her empire awaited her. Adam knew approximately how long it would take for them to carry her to The Grand Hall and so, alone out of the many millions of her subjects, he left those areas deep in the bowels of the metropolis that had been designated as assembly points. He began climbing upwards, retracing the routes he had taken that day, to see why it was that he felt so disturbed.

Chapter 2

AntLand Under Threat

Recognising Adam immediately as an Elder, the assembled ants attempted to part for him, but there was so little room in the passageways that Adam was compelled to force his way through the multitude, his complex joints oscillating in concern. The heat made him feel somewhat disorientated. Standing in a vast tunnel in a part of the metropolis near the surface, he was surprised to find he needed to steady himself. Perhaps, he thought, it was because of his haste, or the fact that the heat generated by so many ants congregating tightly in the depths of the metropolis wafted up and into the uppermost tunnels in which he now stood. Perhaps it was because he was concerned that he had broken protocol: all the other Elders would, by now, have taken up their privileged positions on the stage of The Grand Hall, and his absence would have raised antennae, particularly with AyJay Heartland, who had bitterly opposed Adam's appointment to The Council of Elders. This was an issue he would deal with later. For now, there were greater matters that needed his attention.

He quickened his pace, investigating first the honeydew,

greenfly and ladybird chambers and then the vaults in which dead organic matter was deposited so that it could be used as fertiliser. All was as it should be, except ... As he was about to leave the last of these rooms he paused and, for reasons he could not later explain, felt the need to make a closer analysis of the air. His antennae twitched and jerked as he scanned the odours in the room. He shifted his two large spherical eyes that gave him a wide field of vision as well as the three smaller eyes situated on his forehead. His infrared receivers detected a source of warmth so intense as to be unfamiliar to him. He departed, puzzled, and thought to inspect those parts of the farmland dedicated to the cultivation of fungi. These mushroom gardens, supplying food predominantly for AntLand's larvae, stood eerily silent, devoid of the activity he had become accustomed to. His antennae contracted, pulling, thrusting, twisting as they tested the air, raking over the various scents in an attempt to isolate what he felt was some intrusion. He moved alongside the serried rows of fungi, examining the tiny mushrooms, confused as to what it was that unnerved him. He lingered in the principal room far longer than he knew he should have, aware of some encroachment. What was it?

He pressed on with hesitant, measured movements of his feet, looking into some of those chambers in which seeds, meat and flour were stored. He investigated several rooms in which leaves were cut into tiny pieces then taken to other parts of the farmland where they were chewed by his specialist workers into pulp. He scanned the air. The result was as he had expected. The repulsive odour, whatever its source, whatever its effect, had infiltrated much of the empire. What did it mean? Everywhere he went he was aware of this hint of violation in the air. Was it related to the city's waste products? It couldn't be. He shook his head vigorously in rejection: his team of sanitation workers had, earlier that morning, dumped waste at the designated positions outside the city, as Adam had ensured they did every day since the Queen had elevated him to the position of Elder. Adam retraced the route his sanitation teams had taken; perhaps they had dropped some waste in their haste to complete their work and assemble as close as possible to The Grand Hall. It was unlikely, indeed, unheard of, however ...

Adam stood at the entrance of another chamber. He could barely believe the evidence before him. The empire was meticulous in its removal of those who had passed away. Those who expired – and expire they did, every day, in their hundreds – gave off a chemical that was pungent, unmistakable, unambiguously unlike the odour that perplexed him. Yet here, piled into a room, were thousands of corpses that should have been deposited in the cemetery outside the city. What shocked Adam was not only that strict procedure had been ignored or that so many had passed away ... equally disturbing was the manner of death of some of those dumped in the room. Many had distended abdomens, and roundworms had burst out of the abdominal cavity of several ants and were now feasting on their wretched hosts.

Alarmed that some invisible force had invaded AntLand, Adam inspected the health of the sap-sucking insects that were so vital for the health of the empire. He tapped one with his antennae and the aphid immediately began secreting its honeydew. This calmed Adam's agitated nerves. He gave the aphid an affectionate stroke with one of his antennae and brushed both mandibles tenderly against the flanks of the insect. He stared for a long time at the sap-sucker and, for the first time, considered the blessed existence of the ant: such a contrast to the life of an insect such as this, whose only role was to consume, survive and reproduce. The nutritious excrement it exuded was, admittedly, an important source of food, but the aphid's only motive in serving the empire was that the ants protected it against predatory insects and parasites. This stupid creature, however, had not chosen to be a sap-sucker, just as Adam had not chosen to be an ant. He wondered how it was that some, like him, were born privileged while others were born as imbeciles. Did this aphid, he wondered, have a sap-sucker god it worshipped? Was it aware that the entire universe ended at that mountainous circle enclosing AntLand? Did it know of the existence of AntGod, and that whatever it worshipped, if it worshipped anything at all, was a false god?

Adam was so deep in thought as he started to make his way back to The Grand Hall that he took a wrong turn and became disoriented by the complete lack of chemical pheromonic discharges on the tunnel's walls and its roof. He was considering the disquieting thought that the odour was in some way related to the heat, the absence of secretions and the bizarre disposal of the dead, when he suddenly realised he had gone too far down into the lower depths of the city. What had awoken him from his reveries was the shallow pool of water he found himself standing in. He stopped. The tunnel was under water. He had not journeyed into this part of the city for a long, long time. The entire area had, he saw, become uninhabitable. Water dripped with an unnerving continuity. He cleaned his sensory mechanism then tested some of the walls and cavities and the ceiling: there was not the slightest evidence of pheromones anywhere. He used the claw of one of his forelegs to rake at the walls and floor, then tested these also with his antennae. The entire area had obviously been abandoned, evacuated long ago. How long? And why had he not been informed? And what was the source of all this water? He departed quickly.

Making his way to the front of The Grand Hall, Adam took his reserved position amongst the other Elders and waited for the Queen's entry. The position reserved for him was next to AyJay Heartland, the Queen's Senior Advisor and ChairAnt of The Council of Elders, who was responsible for those workers who removed the remains of the expired from the city. Adam immediately informed him of the dead he had seen in the chamber. AyJay Heartland did not speak. He cast Adam a sideways, cold, unblinking glare. Adam did not return his stare of admonition.

AyJay Heartland summoned Gredo, an Assistant-Elder who was seen as one of his strongest supporters. Gredo responded quickly to AyJay's summons, approaching then throwing his body into a military rigidity, his antennae quivering excitedly. The close contact of their inclined heads and the movement of their antennae indicated some secretive exchange. Assistant-Elder Gredo cast a long look at Adam out of the corner of one of his eyes before scurrying out of The Grand Hall to do Elder AyJay's bidding, accompanied by several Imperial Runners.

After several moments AyJay spoke. There was a decided

pause between each word. 'You are late. Council Elders are expected to set an example.'

'Yes, Elder AyJay, but I needed ——'

'You needed to be here waiting for the Queen's entry. I do not expect to have to engage in a dispute with new members of The Council when they are clearly in the wrong. Every single one of our longstanding Elders arrived on this platform at the stipulated time while you, our youngest, took it upon yourself to interfere in my responsibilities. The disposal of the dead is my concern, not yours. This is unacceptable behaviour, Elder Adam. Your conduct will be discussed at our next meeting. I require you to respond appropriately.'

Adam frowned, puzzled at the ChairAnt's words.

'I said, I require a response.'

'I apologise for my lateness, Elder AyJay. But you need to know that the strange odour I detected in all the chambers and tunnels some weeks ago has inexplicably intensified, and that the lower depths of the empire are under water. There are chambers which are uninhabitable and ——'

'The maintenance of those chambers is not your responsibility. I know you have been concerned about some odour. You have informed me on two other occasions. Do you think I have forgotten? Are you questioning my memory, young Elder Adam? I wonder: could this concern of yours be related to any ambition you might have? Why is it that no other Elder shares your anxieties? You are creating problems where none exist and you are impinging upon areas designated as the responsibilities of others.'

'My concerns are related to the heat and this strange odour which has suddenly got worse and ——'

'I know what your concerns are, Elder Adam. And I know who and what you are. You are impudent. You are interfering in areas not allotted to your care. You, the youngest ever Elder in our history are, I see, eager to assume roles above your station. You are eager to show yourself as someone who sees what we, apparently, are unable to see. How and why the Queen appointed you without consulting me is a complete mystery to me. I can only assume that you have bewitched her with your youthful charm. Be warned, Elder Adam. Refrain. Re-*frain*. And as for what you said earlier, there are no dead in the city.' His razor-edged mandibles opened and closed.

'I would never presume to tell you, the Queen's most trusted confidant, how you should carry out your duties.'

'The waterlogged tunnels are of no concern. They will be drained. Again, I must repeat myself: this is my responsibility, Elder Adam, not yours. *Not ... yours.* Do I make myself clear? If so, reply by saying: "You make yourself clear, ChairAnt".'

Adam replied as he had been instructed.

'Good. And, I repeat, there are no dead in the city. I trust you will not cause undue concern amongst our citizenry on this special day by disseminating false rumours.'

'But, I've seen with my own eyes.'

'I suggest you make an inspection of that chamber after the Queen's address. You have my permission to do so. You will see that I am correct. I am quite sure Assistant-Elder Gredo will confirm what I just said. And once you have done so, you will see with your own eyes that you are in error. Indeed, on this occasion I would strongly encourage you to conduct such an inspection. I trust that the matter will not need pursuing. Now, look at our subjects, chattering to one another, taking liberties as a result of my having to conduct this conversation with you in order that I might correct your behaviour. You have caused us to set a bad example.'

Adam was silent.

AyJay Heartland looked at Adam with eyes as black as coal. 'I have encouraged you to make your inspection. I have asked you whether the matter will end when you see that there are no dead in the chamber. You have not responded to my suggestions.'

'I was merely informing you of the oversight of your workers. I meant no disrespect.'

'And let this be the final occasion when you raise your tiresome concerns about some non-existent odour.'

AyJay Heartland raised his abdomen to indicate his anger. He rubbed his legs together while glaring hard into Adam's eyes until the intimidated Adam shifted his gaze into the assembled multitude, sweeping his eyes across the heaving mass of patient black ants who waited obediently for their Queen. Standing perfectly still, Young Nano, The Watching Ant, was, of course, watching him. Nano responded to Adam's distress by dipping his antennae to the ground and moving them from side to side, using some of the chemicals at his disposal to expel a message from a gland at the bottom of his jaw. The vapour spread in a direct line to Adam. It stated: *I know.*

Chapter 3

A Spy Infiltrates

It was two months earlier – and three weeks after he had been appointed as an Elder – when Adam had first taken note of this peculiar odour. He had been on his regular rounds, ensuring the wellbeing of every room, cavity, chamber and vault falling under his care, and was in the agricultural section of the metropolis, when he became distracted from his observations by the sudden intrusion of several of his workers. It was clear from the frantic movements of their antennae, the chaotic spillage of their indecipherable chemical discharges and the confused movements of their feet as they made quick, short steps around him that something terrible had occurred.

He was given reports of a disastrous event. After a raid in The Eternal Valley, his 30,000 hunters had returned to the city with a vast harvest of insects. One bee, however, which had been dragged into the city, hauled down the main thoroughfare and into the abattoir, where it was to be dismembered, had escaped from the butcher-ants. An enemy combatant was roaming at will within their very metropolis! The rogue insect needed to be caught and killed. Lives were in danger, as was the reputation of Adam Ant, who was responsible for the hunters. Adam immediately summoned his most senior advisors.

Time was, he told them, of the essence. Under no circumstances was this insect to escape the metropolis alive. He issued his instructions. Every hunter, forager and scout was to assist in the chase, doubling the amount of pheromones left in their tracks to ensure that this bee was not able to contaminate their smell. Three hundred workers were to remove larva from one of the many nurseries then extract the glue each lava secreted. These workers were to use this glue to create sticky silk barriers across stipulated sections of the main thoroughfare, thus inhibiting the bee from flying at will in the metropolis. One thousand foragers were sent to The Imperial Gate; two thousand were instructed to use every single secretory gland in their abdomen, head and legs to emit as powerful a smell and taste as they could, communicating to all the necessity of bringing this hunt to a quick and successful end. Dense phalanxes of ants were immediately marched in various directions to be at the ready to kill the bee once it was found. Scents transmitting a call to arms poured like a rolling fog through the tunnels, pathways, chambers, vaults and galleries, the fearful ants receiving this notice of danger trembling with such agitation that they beat the ground with the end of their abdomen, producing an enormous quantity of aroused and alarmed pheromones.

The initial reports were not encouraging. With the antpower Adam had assembled he had expected an immediate sighting and a rapid entrapment and dispatch of the creature. Why was it taking so long? After all, did they not have the bee isolated in one section of the city?

Adam rushed to the main exit points and watched as his workers held larvae in their mandibles, shutting off each opening with walls of silken glue. When all had been enclosed Adam retreated into the hastily-organised tactics room, where he was scheduled to receive his first report. This was interrupted, however, when a dozen ants, ignoring protocol, burst into the chamber. They were waving their antennae all at once, releasing distress pheromones. The bee, they cried, the bee had broken through one of the larva walls! The bee was nowhere to be found! What to do? What to do?

A runner was sent immediately to those guarding The Imperial Gate, who informed him that the bee had not tried to escape, that there had, in fact, been no sighting of the bee. It was still in the city, hiding.

Adam walked back and forth in the tactics room, thinking, thinking. It was possible that this bee had not been poisoned by his hunters but instead was found, seemingly lifeless and thought to be dead, and brought to the city as carrion. Was that the case? Perhaps there was some ruse at play here. But what? To infiltrate the city, yes, the reason being ... to kill the Queen?

He immediately emitted Pheromones of Utmost Urgency, a recourse an Elder took only for extreme emergencies. If the life of the Queen was at risk, so was that of the entire empire. New directions were given. Ten thousand ants were sent to guard The Royal Chamber. The egg and larvae rooms had their number of workers vastly increased to protect the young. Every network of galleries, chambers and vaults was methodically and meticulously searched. Escape passages were immediately made narrow so that the bee could be isolated. Adam and his advisors were poring over the map of the entire city imprinted in their heads when a runner delivered the shocking news: there had been several sightings of the bee in the nurseries and the farmlands.

Adam decided to take personal charge in the field itself. He rushed to the egg, larvae and pupae rooms. One of the distressed nursemaids informed him that the bee had knocked over the guards, entered one of the rooms, ill-treated several of the youngsters and then flown off. None of the youngsters, however, had been killed. This was a puzzle. What did it mean?

The Elder took his advisors to the nearby farmlands, which were in the centre of the metropolis and close to The Queen's Chamber so that produce for the larvae could be easily accessed. A traumatised worker stated he had seen the bee, seen it himself, detected it with his own antennae and so was able to say that this loathsome creature was either so terrified that it did not know what it was doing, or it was on some sort of fact-finding mission. It had, the worker said, entered several of the largest storerooms, the biggest being 1,000 antbodies in length and 100 antbodies high, and appeared to examine the fungus gardens. The bee seemed to taste – taste! a thing unheard of in a bee – the leaves, compost and fungi. From there it had flown into those areas set aside for livestock, laid eyes on AntLand's thousands of aphids, caterpillars, ladybirds and greenflies, then departed.

The bee, Adam was relieved to hear, had made no attempt to approach The Queen's Chamber.

It had, he thought, flown to so many parts of the city that

it now had knowledge of AntLand's formidable earthworks and the direction of its many tunnels. It had even flown, one report stated, thousands of antbodies down to the waterlogged subterranean rooms.

Report after report came to Adam. Sightings had been made in larders, the vast seed and fungus chambers that contained enough food to withstand a twelve month drought. But bees did not consume fungi and seeds. It was seen in certain livestock galleries. But what interest did it have in their flocks of mealy bugs and aphids, kept for their meat, or in the leaf-hoppers, kept for their secretions? Was this, Adam thought, a deranged bee, frightened out of its wits, trying desperately to escape what it surely realised was certain death were it to be apprehended?

And then came the news he had dreaded. The bee had burst through the silk-secreted barrier glued to The Imperial Gate. A fierce battle had ensued. Some brave warriors had attached themselves to the bee as it made its escape into the outside world. They were seen to be furiously injecting the insect while it was in flight.

By now every inhabitant of AntLand would know that he, Adam Ant, the rising star of The Council of Elders, had been forced to invoke the Pheromones of Utmost Urgency. The bee might have survived the repeated stinging of the ants who had heroically attached themselves to the beast while it was in flight. If that was the case, it had to be recaptured. It had to found, killed and brought back in triumph to the metropolis. He had to show AntLand that his recent elevation to the position of an Elder had been justified. Adam summoned half a million of his foragers, hunters and scouts. They assembled in a vast circle outside the city. They stood in heightened anticipation in the warmth, waiting for instructions under a pale sky and a blinding sun – and so it was that while they waited for Adam's orders, he happened to take note of a particularly pungent odour being emitted from the air vents of the metropolis. He pushed aside his curiosity and gave his instructions. His ants fanned out with orders to scour the surrounding bushland to a distance of 5,000 antbodies.

Adam caught up with his workers. Some had broken into groups, others into columns. Most had maintained a great chain, 100 antbodies thick, a black swarm searching every hole, every rut, the interior of every dead, hollow branch. They moved at a quick pace, covering 2,500 antbody lengths by midafternoon. They found the bee struggling to maintain its hold on the branch of a shrub. Ignoring pleas from his subordinates not to risk his life, Adam took after it, scurrying along branch after branch until he stood directly above the insect. Tens of thousands of his followers watched in horror and amazement as he released his hold on a leaf and dropped onto an eye of the bee and bit it repeatedly. As the bee writhed in agony, Adam did what no other ant had ever been known to do: he slid into the bee's mouth. He used the three infrared eyes on his forehead to find the insect's throat then slithered down its gullet, biting repeatedly into the tender flesh. The bee fell from the branch and onto the ground, by which time Adam had journeyed into its bowels. He exited the bee through its anus and ran around to fire formic acid into its good eye until, moments later, reinforcements arrived.

When the sun began to set, the ants commenced their long march home. The bee was carried aloft by fifty ants in procession, with Adam walking alone, like some conquering hero, at their rear. They entered The Imperial Gate in glory.

AyJay Heartland looked on, his pheromones smouldering.

The next day the Queen issued a public statement commending Adam Ant for his bravery, crediting him with having saved AntLand from calamity. The statement was transmitted by Royal Pheromones, an unusual honour that further enraged AyJay Heartland. Adam was summoned to The Royal Chamber to receive the Queen's personal expression of gratitude.

Upon the conclusion of his audience with the Queen, Adam Ant, recalling the pungent odour he had detected the previous day, made his way alone to The Imperial Gate, taking note that the contrast in temperature between the warm air within the metropolis and the bracing air outside prompted the warmer air to rise. He returned to one of the many surface vents and felt the flow of the warm odour.

As soon as Adam was back underground, he sought an immediate meeting with AyJay Heartland.

'Tell me,' the ChairAnt said, once Adam had expressed his concern, 'what you are implying.'

'I'm not sure, Elder AyJay, but I sense our metropolis is acting as a giant respiratory system. Our paths and passages, our arteries and thoroughfares have become a means for pumping out a strange odour through our many vents. But it's the effect of this odour on us, our aphids, our caterpillars and the air we breathe that concerns me.'

'An odour.'

'Yes.'

'You are concerned about an odour.'

'Yes, my ChairAnt.'

'You said that you are not sure.'

'Yes.'

'What, exactly, are you not sure about?'

'I'd taken note of a change in the air some time ago, but it's recently become more intense. It seems to have transformed into something new. I'm not sure what this means.'

'I see. You are not sure. You have sought a meeting with Her Majesty's Senior Advisor and ChairAnt of her Council of Elders to inform him that our farmlands, our nurseries, we ourselves – breathing, living AntLanders – are producing an odour.'

Silence.

'Your so-called heroism has affected your judgement, Adam Ant. What, however, could one expect from someone who has risen above his station, one with so little experience all right-thinking AntLanders are wondering what it is that you have done to be appointed as an Elder. You are not sure. I, however, am sure of this: while you might have impressed the Queen, we would not have had a problem with that bee had you ensured it was dead prior to having it dragged into our metropolis; and while I do not doubt that you entered into the body of that bee, it was only after it had been disabled by numerous, much more heroic ants than you, who injected it with our potent formic acid. And now you are attempting to distinguish yourself by raising questions about – what is it, again? Air, is it? Leave me, Adam Ant.'

Chapter 4

The Queen's Address

AyJay Heartland walked to the centre of the platform. He raised one of his front feet as a sign that he was about to speak. A great silence fell on the gathering. 'As the most senior member of the Queen's Council of Elders, I propose that we take the opportunity on this, the most auspicious of occasions, to display the love we feel for our Queen. It could well be that you never set eyes on her again. It could well be that there never will be another occasion when you will be able, with one voice, to show her your devotion. I propose, therefore, that we honour our Queen with the title, Our Great Mother. The term expresses the unbreakable bond between us and her; it represents our boundless loyalty and, most of all, our obedience. Indicate your support for my proposal by acclamation.'

A million or so black ants in The Grand Hall responded as one, vigorously rubbing their antennae and other body parts together. A reverberating effusion of pheromones was emitted from those who had been honoured by being selected to gather in the hall. It was immediately absorbed then secreted by the ants who had congregated in strict formation in the many passageways, rooms, chambers and vaults, and on the bridges and archways leading off this vast chamber, all of which trembled with the reaction of the Queen's loyal subjects. Labyrinthine tunnels and cavities far from The Grand Hall echoed loud and long with their joyful cries.

AyJay Heartland made erect his antennae. The ants responded by falling silent.

'Prepare yourselves for our Queen's entry,' said the ChairAnt.

A hundred ants, carrying the litter on which the Queen inclined, emerged from a side vestibule. The moment she appeared the assembled ants drew a mighty, collective, audible breath, expressing, perhaps, their jubilation, or their shock at the mere sight of their sovereign. They prostrated themselves before her in obeisance, touching the ground with the top of their heads. Many were so overcome they expired. Other ants lost consciousness or fell into convulsions. Adam looked sideways at AyJay Heartland, noting that the Queen's Senior Advisor had bowed his head but had not prostrated himself. AyJay returned his stare. The ChairAnt's heavy-lidded eyes fell upon the younger Elder. Adam tried to stare down AyJay Heartland. He failed. He noted the sudden emission of self-righteous, self-satisfied pheromones from the ChairAnt's abdomen.

The Queen was assisted in climbing down from the litter. She approached the centre of the platform and stood there for a long time without making any effort to communicate to her subjects.

After several moments, she said: 'Raise your heads.'

She scanned their faces. Few could summon the courage

to look into her eyes. Finally, she began her address. Her choice of words, even the syntax, had Adam thinking that her speech might have been written by AyJay Heartland. What puzzled him was a hint of indecisiveness in her manner. He watched her carefully. She did, indeed, seem uncharacteristically hesitant. What did this mean?

'Aeons ago,' she said, 'a giant rock from the heavens was sent by AntGod Himself to create the universe, which we know as The Eternal Valley. This rock also created The Sacred Circle of Cliffs. The universe was dark, lifeless and forbidding for an incalculable period of time until we were guided here. AntLand was chosen. We, all, were chosen.

'Every ant that has ever lived has seen out his life in our empire. This is all there is.'

The Queen stopped. Adam Ant stiffened his antennae. He absorbed the Queen's transmitted message. The odour he detected was one of ... What? Vacillation? Irresolution?

AyJay Heartland approached the Queen, directing several chemical signals of his own solely to her. He then resumed his position. She returned to what Adam was now certain was a speech that AyJay Heartland had prepared for her.

'Beyond the mountaintops lies what Elder AyJay has told us is The Great Darkness and what I refer to as The NoWorld. AntLand is, then, an extraordinary place, carrying alone the weight of divine expectations. In the design of The Eternal Valley we, and we alone, are here to fulfil AntGod's commands.

'What, we ask you, is our purpose as a species?

'Three hundred and eighty-eight months ago we carved out alone a single room in which we raised our first brood of workers whom we nourished with our own saliva. These workers gathered food to feed the next generation of ants, whom we appointed as either foragers or builders of our underground world. We continued producing subjects, devoting our lives so that AntLand could fulfil her mission.'

The Queen paused. She looked from one side of the hall to the other. She waited. And while Adam watched, so did Young Nano.

'And what is this mission? It is to be fruitful and multiply. So it is written in The Holy AntBook; so it has been done.

'Growth is, therefore, good, otherwise we would not, for so many consecutive months, have grown until we now number over thirty million subjects. Before the rock fell into The Eternal Valley, there were no ants. Now our presence and domination of the universe is so pervasive that the last 388 months have been given a name by our ChairAnt: The Antocene Period. This is irrefutable evidence that AntLand was made for us, rather than we being made for AntLand, and why we have no enemies that threaten us.

'However, The Holy AntBook tells us that dust we are and to dust we shall return. Our mission is, therefore, one of urgency. If the history of AntLand has been one of continual growth, and if this growth is the perpetual fulfilment of AntGod's command, then we must accept this as a divine commandment. We believe this. We say again, we believe this.'

And thirty million ants responded as one: 'This we believe!'

Adam, however, had taken note of the anxious pheromones discharging from the Queen's legs. The Elders, sensing her apprehension, looked from one to the other.

Adam raked the air with the end of one of his mandibles. He detected once again her ambivalence, her wavering effusions, her scepticism – nay, her cynicism. Looking askance at AyJay Heartland and detecting his haughtiness, Adam wondered whether the Queen had been given any say at all in the content of her speech.

'We began,' she continued, 'as simple hunter-gatherers. We learnt to tame the inferior creatures made for us, milk them for their honeydew and breed them for their meat. We have learnt the skills of agriculture. We are The Eternal Valley's superorganism. Should we not be proud of our dominion of the universe? Is it not an issue of truth that we accept the reality of our superiority and see this, too, as a Divine Commandment? We believe this.'

'This we believe!'

Adam cast another sideways look at AyJay Heartland. He saw the smug look on the Elder's face, absorbed the self-congratulatory pheromones exuded from various parts of his exoskeleton. What was the Queen's aim in her speech? Clearly, the aged ChairAnt knew something that Adam and the other Elders did not.

'We have a unity of purpose that is remarkable and unmatched in any other species. We have about us a *finesse* ...'

It was precisely at this moment that Adam knew, without any doubt at all, that the Queen's address had, indeed, been written by AyJay. For who else but the ChairAnt used such a word.

'... in all that we do. We are the antithesis of the self-centred spider who lives a solitary life, and of the caterpillar who is not genetically capable of achieving our level of cooperation. Beloved subjects, we have been able to imagine a bigger and better world as we grew. What we imagined, we created. We have subdued the natural world to our will. And yet, in following AntGod's commandment that we grow, we have made of our metropolis a place that is becoming overpopulated. Our problem, however, is antmade. Therefore, it can be solved by antkind. No problem of ant destiny is beyond the ant. We believe this.'

'This we believe!'

'And we have AntGod helping us, giving us clear guidance as to the solving of this problem. Beloved AntLanders, you will have noticed that ever since the temperature began to rise, the number of eggs we have been producing has increased. Why is this so? We do not know. We do not ask. AntGod has willed it so. With the overcrowding of our metropolis and the ever-increasing number of offspring we produce, what is clear is that we have been given a sign. Just as growth has characterised AntLand from the day when we created The Royal Chamber and laid our first egg, now we have been instructed to grow in a way that will bring us greater glory, that will enable us to eat better food, cultivate more land and graze more livestock for our growing population of eggs, larvae and pupae. More chambers, more power, more wealth, and all achieved without needing to create armed forces. It is our destiny, beloved, that we become bigger, better, best. We believe this. We ask you: do you also believe?'

'This we believe!'

Adam Ant was horrified. More power? And why this reference to armed forces when they had no enemy? He looked across at AyJay Heartland and saw, and knew.

'It is for this reason we have had you gather in The Grand Hall. The universe was once a world without pity. We survived and multiplied and dominated because we have a natural inclination to grow and prosper. In twelve months' time, we celebrate the 400th month since AntLand's founding. Preparations to commemorate that day have already begun. Apart from traditional celebratory events, the occasion will be marked by the parading of the holy grains of sand I alighted upon when first being guided to this valley and the completion of the largest building programme conducted since our founding, one initially proposed and relentlessly pursued by my Senior Advisor and ChairAnt of The Council of Elders, AyJay Heartland. Beginning immediately, what will take twelve months to complete will stand as the wonder of the universe. Our beloved AyJay Heartland will oversee the construction of what is to be known as The Royal Tower, which will be positioned on top of our city, quadrupling the size of our empire. We say that again: we embark tomorrow on increasing the size of AntLand fourfold. No longer shall we expand by going down into the bowels of the earth, but up, always up, higher and higher. We aim to be bigger, better, the best. When construction has been completed our city will be a symbol of our towering aspiration and sophistication. Let us build a tower that will be a rival to the snow-capped Sacred Circle of Cliffs themselves, so that we are ...?'

'Bigger! Better! Best!'

'This can be done. This will be done. This we believe!'

'This we believe!'

'AyJay Heartland ... rise!'

AyJay stood on his rear legs to receive a frenzied response

from the hall. He cocked his head high, raised one antenna and gave what seemed to Adam a wave of acknowledgement, designed not as an expression of gratitude but as a way of prolonging the applause. When Adam detected at the tips of his antennae an unambiguous and sudden release of arrogance and pomposity from glands all over AyJay Heartland's body, he had no doubt that this mad scheme had originated from this old, proud, vainglorious ant.

AyJay Heartland resumed his position and, detecting Adam's horror at what the Queen had just announced, turned to face him. He looked at Adam with detached eyes, daring him once again to maintain eye contact. Adam did not flinch. He did not shrink from AyJay Heartland's challenge. The older ant gave way beneath the young Elder's provocation. Neither was now in doubt. Their relationship had permanently shifted. Humiliated by his backdown, AyJay Heartland tensed his body, forced an emission of hostile pheromones from several glands in his legs, head and thorax then turned his surly eyes back upon Adam.

What happened next wiped the menace from AyJay Heartland's face. The Queen turned from her subjects to look at her Elders. With the acclamation of the ants for AyJay Heartland rising to a pitch, the ChairAnt assumed that the Queen had turned to face *him,* to acknowledge *his* triumph by resting her eyes and antennae upon *him.* What she did, however, was to search out Adam. Her contemplation of her youngest Elder agitated AyJay Heartland. Her long consideration of him, the affectionate movements of her legs and antennae and the many effusions of tender pheromones infuriated the ChairAnt. AyJay Heartland rose and approached the front of the stage. What, Adam wondered, was going on? Why had the Queen paused in her speech? What was she trying to communicate to him? What did her thoughtful deliberation of him mean? And why had AyJay Heartland risen so quickly to his feet? Was AyJay about to bring to an end the gathering?

If that had been his intention, he was thwarted when the Queen resumed speaking.

The assembled ants fell silent. AyJay Heartland stood beside her, looking unmistakenly confused and indecisive.

'The time has also come,' she said, 'to create a new city-state.'

The Queen paused. AyJay jerked his head towards her then back to Adam, a look of alarm on his face. Adam immediately knew that the words Her Majesty was about to deliver had been neither prepared, sanctioned nor even discussed with her Senior Advisor nor, indeed, with The Council.

'In twelve months' time,' she said, 'a female, specially selected by us, will fly out of our metropolis. A male, also selected by us, will pursue her. Once she has mated with her pursuer, she will proceed to a site in The Eternal Valley upon which a colony will be established. The Elder responsible for choosing the site and who will also, for the first time in our history, survey The Eternal Valley, is an ant who knows the plains better than any other: our most recently appointed Elder, the Royal Forager and Grand Protector of Food Supplies, Adam Ant.'

The Queen had taken all by surprise, none more so than Adam. He was not even aware that she was encouraging him to stand so that he could receive the applause of her subjects.

The creation of a colony, he knew, was an act of wisdom. The metropolis had long been overcrowded. And so he turned to look at AyJay Heartland, whose antennae were violently convulsing in angry spasms. How would the ChairAnt respond?

The Queen raised herself as far as she could on her rear legs and announced that Elder Adam Ant was also being groomed personally by her to undertake an even more important leadership role, that he would assume the positions of Senior Advisor and ChairAnt of her Council of Elders when the time came, many months in the future, for the aging AyJay Heartland to step down from his positions. Assistant-Elder Gredo, AyJay's protégé, sat bolt upright in surprise, his antennae stiffening in agitated indignation. He stared helplessly at AyJay who, caught off guard by the Queen's announcement, threw a sharp look at the bewildered Adam. The decision, however, was received with a cry of approval by her subjects, who rubbed their antennae together in jubilation.

The Queen called Adam to come forward. And while receiving AntLand's rapturous reception, the Queen said to him: 'AyJay Heartland has made of my chamber a prison. Listen carefully. This building programme must not proceed. Find me a suitable location for a colony. Leave. Leave as soon as you can. Take Zekiel the Wise with you. Choose 100 JourneyAnts to accompany you. There must be no delay. Adam Ant, do you undertand? This might be the last occasion when I am able to speak to you. I need to know you understand what has to be done. Do you?'

'Yes, Your Majesty.'

'And one more thing, Elder Adam: as soon as you have departed the metropolis, inspect our waste dumps. Take a reading. If you are able to gain access to me, inform me on your return if there is any similarity between the odours discharged from the waste dumps and those from your fungus farms.'

'Then you, too, have noted that ——'

'Depart, Elder Adam.'

As she was being carried back to her chamber in her litter, AyJay Heartland approached Adam. He bent his head low so that his rigid antennae were almost touching Adam's. 'You do not know what you do. She does not know what she does. A colony? One that in time will seek independence, that will, in time, even challenge our authority? Insanity! And you, of all the Elders, chosen to succeed me? When it was you who put our entire empire at risk when you brought into our midst a live bee? You knew of the Queen's plans, Elder Adam, you knew and you chose not to inform me. You are not to leave the metropolis. That is a direct order. Do not cross me, Adam Ant. You do so at your peril. Do not think that the Queen will be able to protect you from my wrath. You have been warned.' The Elder's exoskeleton gleamed with indignation and fury.

Custom decreed that AyJay Heartland, as the Queen's Senior Advisor and ChairAnt, accompany Her Majesty to her chamber. Despite this convention, Adam saw AyJay Heartland rush off in the opposite direction. Where, Adam wondered, was he going?

Adam remained on the platform as the ants left the hall, a black ocean of AntLanders exiting quickly and quietly. He was still standing there long after The Grand Hall had been emptied. He had not sought this honour. Truth to tell, had he been asked and given the choice, he might well have declined. In one stroke Her Majesty had made AyJay Heartland and Assistant-Elder Gredo his bitter and dangerous life-long enemies.

But there was more. He was thinking. The Queen had made reference to the rising temperature. He was not the only one, then, who was aware of this. She had also said that she was producing more eggs than was usually the case. Adam had not been aware of this. As an Elder he should have been told. At any one of The Council of Elders meetings, they should have all been informed. Why was there secrecy surrounding this rise in their numbers? And if that were the case, where were they? He had certainly not seen any evidence of a more than anticipated, regulated rise in their population, one designed to replace those ants who died.

Her Majesty had then said: Why is this so? We do not know. *We do not ask.*

But why should we not ask?

And, AyJay Heartland was the one who had the Queen instigate the cry of 'bigger, better, best', and yet, they were the *only* ants in The Eternal Valley. Better, then, than whom? As there were no other ants, why make the comparison when no-one would consider for a moment comparing them to the inferior creatures? The idea was ludicrous. And as for striving to be the best ... Hadn't the Queen herself said that no other species was better organised, more sophisticated, more civilised than they? The refrain, enthusiastically, wildly, *thoughtlessly* accepted by all but Adam Ant, made no sense.

While he stood there thinking on these things, Zekiel, the Royal Sage, arrived with a message from the Queen: 'Do not return to your chambers. Follow Zekiel the Wise in all that he says. Depart unseen, Adam Ant, and as a matter of urgency. Zekiel will show you the way.'

Adam and Zekiel went to the rooms where Adam had seen the dead. The bodies had been removed. He licked one of his antennae then wiped it clean and dry on a bristled spur on his elbow. Vibrating it here and there over the ground, he was not at all surprised to detect an angry chemical discharge. It was unmistakable. It had come from AyJay Heartland. When the ChairAnt should have escorted the Queen to her chamber, he had, instead, ensured the removal of the dead so that evidence of – of what? his incompetence? the effect of the rise in temperature? – could not be used against him. If Adam were to tell anyone what he had seen earlier that day, would anyone believe him?

And Zekiel, absorbing Adam's pheromones, said: 'I believe you, Master.'

And what, he wondered, would the consequences be for the Queen?

And Zekiel, knowing what Adam was thinking, said: 'She is under guard, Master, and will remain so until The Royal Tower has been completed.'

Chapter 5

Construction of The Royal Tower Begins

'We must depart under cover of night, Master,' said Zekiel. 'There is a passage known only to the Queen and myself, created long ago for any emergency exit the Queen might require.'

'Not yet, Zekiel. It's long been estimated that there are about 80,000 antbody lengths between The Imperial Gate and the base of The Sacred Circle of Cliffs. If this is correct, it means we'll be absent from the metropolis for at least six months. I must ensure there'll be no shortfall in produce from the farms and livestock in my absence and that the empire's reserves are adequate in case of an emergency. The Queen has also instructed me to take readings.'

'I fear,' said Zekiel, 'that the ChairAnt might have ordered The Imperial Runners to apprehend you.'

'Then we must hurry. Come, let's inspect The Royal Farmlands.'

His anxieties were confirmed when one of his senior workers, casting apprehensive pheromones haphazardly here and there, skittered to Adam's left and right as he informed the Elder that it was not only the fungi that had been growing faster, bigger and heavier than was usual for that time. Adam frowned, rubbing his mandibles together in an agitated fashion. This senior worker took Adam and Zekiel to the honeydew fermentation chambers, where he apprised them of the recent problem: much of what they harvested had grown so quickly that its bitterness precluded consumption. This senior then led them to the rooms in which the aphids, mayflies and mealy bugs were bred as a food supply. The breeder responsible for this particular source told them that the insects were emerging from their eggs earlier than in previous seasons. Adam asked the breeder and his senior worker why this was so, but neither ant was able to offer an explanation. Adam asked to be taken to those vaults in which anal secretions were collected from the ladybirds and greenflies that the empire bred specifically for that purpose, only to be told that many of the newborns were growing so quickly they had developed deformities.

'And our snails?'

'The same, Master,' the worker told Adam.

'What's happening, Zekiel? What's going on?'

Adam Ant wondered whether this was a temporary aberration or whether the pattern of growth in plant and creature had become permanently unpredictable. Everywhere he and Zekiel went they were able to detect the odour Adam had brought to the attention of AyJay Heartland. Was this smell in any way related to the heat and the erratic behaviour of the empire's crops and livestock?

'It's getting worse, Zekiel. It's become more intense than when I first detected it. What does this mean?'

Zekiel made a brief, unintelligible response.

'What, Zekiel? Finish what you were about to say.'

Zekiel remained silent, standing sombre and solemn, his eyes and antennae heavy in thought.

'Zekiel, you must share your thoughts with me.'

'I am not sure what to make of this, Master. I do not know what to think. Or, rather, I do not know whether those thoughts I quickly dismiss have any substance.'

'And why dismiss them? Why do you think they might not have substance?'

'We must hurry, Master. If my worst fears are realised, we have little time before we are apprehended. Listen to your Queen.'

'No. Not yet. Follow me.'

Adam and Zekiel inspected the chamber in which specialist ants sliced leaves into rectangular pieces prior to crushing and shaping them into pasties, after which they would align the cakes on a bed of ant excrement, keeping them moist and sanitised with their saliva. Part of the chamber was in disarray. Some of the leaves had been cut into circles, others into squares. Many of the cakes had not been sanitised. Some of the refuse had not been dumped outside the metropolis. Adam brushed a sample of an unidentifiable growth on one of the leaves with a claw and licked it.

'What do you detect, Master?'

Adam scanned several of the pasties, increasing the vibrations of his antennae until they had achieved their utmost reception capacity, shaking and quivering to such an extent that the gust he created drew whatever floated in that chamber towards him. He ceased the vibrations. The sickening scents had him release pheromones of acute alarm.

He turned to face the old ant, his pheromones intensifying with every passing moment.

They inspected that quarter where the newly-hatched ants were provided with antcare. Adam knew that they needed to be maintained at a constant temperature to ensure healthy development. He turned to Zekiel, who attended these young. 'You didn't respond when I asked you what is happening. You remained silent when I asked you what these changes mean. I was aware of some alterations in growth and behaviour, but not of their extent. I've not taken care of this, Zekiel! It had fallen to me and I've been careless. I should have acted, long ago, when I first knew something was amiss! What have I done? Oh, dear AntGod! Zekiel? Speak. I'm absorbing your pheromones. I feel your disquiet. And please don't tell me we can speak of this afterwards.'

'There might not be an afterwards, Master.'

'That is your response? No, that won't do. Impose your brevity on others, not upon me!"

'You are familiar, Master, with the word "thereafter". Forwards or afterwards, there where we go on the Queen's mission we shall see what "after" entails. It could be no more than a sound.'

'You refer to the source? The inception? No riddles, Zekiel!'

'Both provenance and conclusion, Master.'

'Oh, Zekiel, must you speak so ambiguously?'

Adam had always had a particular affection for Zekiel. He had noted long ago how Zekiel's calm and grave antennae moved with a delicate grace. Despite Zekiel's lowly birth, he had an aristocratic bearing. His still demeanour conveyed his quiet authority. His temperate views and the understanding emanating from his large, melancholy eyes were acknowledged by many, particularly the Queen. Adam had taken note on many an occasion when Zekiel would offer no opinion on issues being discussed when in company, so reluctant was he to impose himself upon others; later, however, he would give to Adam his balanced, well-considered view, one Adam always respected and, more often than not, adopted. On the rare occasion when this old ant did offer an opinion on some topic in company, all would fall silent, their eyes and antennae turned towards him in deference.

'Forgive me, Master, I do not intend to be vague or ambiguous. Allow me to tell you this. Of late, I have had to move eggs, larvae and pupae far more frequently from one brood chamber to another than had been previously the case.'

'Because of the extreme fluctuations in temperature.'

'Yes, Master.' Zekiel shuffled his six feet on the ground. Both his antennae performed troubled, slow half-circles.

'You're uneasy, old worker, as uneasy as I am,' Adam Ant said. 'I'm looking at a face of stone.'

He reached out to Zekiel. The older ant responded: the Elder and The Royal Sage stood with their antennae entwined in intimate counsel, an olfactory message passing from one to the other with some ambiguity.

'Zekiel the Wise, what do you want to say to me? You hesitate to tell me what disturbs you. I feel that you're consumed by sadness. Tell me what you know. Tell me what you fear. Speak plainly.'

The ant lowered his head. 'When it is hot, I organise those

over whom I have responsibility to transport water from mouth to mouth. The water is regurgitated onto the walls and floor of the nursery. As a consequence, the temperature is lowered. You know this, Master. It is what we have always done. What you do not know is that recently we have had to undertake such an exercise more regularly than ever before. If I may ask you, Master, to take note of the word *ever*. But there is more. Our broods of young ants used to locate themselves, without any guidance from us, into concentric circles. The broods instinctively knew where to position themselves. The larger larvae on the outer edge have lately been moving into the centre.'

'But … but why? This is unprecedented. I'm correct, am I not, Zekiel?'

'You are.'

'And the eggs in the centre?'

'Crushed.'

'By the larger larvae?'

'Yes.'

'What of the pupae in the middle?'

'There is no order. We find them everywhere: close to the centre, in the outer ring, but rarely, if ever, in the middle, where they should be.'

'Why? Why had I not taken note of this?'

Silence.

'Is there something you want to say? In confidence?'

'Forgive me, Elder Adam.' The old worker stood with his head bowed.

'Forgive you? But why? What have you done?'

'It is not what I have done; it is what I know. There are

occasions when knowledge itself occasions remorse.'

'I don't understand, Zekiel.'

'The pressure on our metropolis can only be alleviated by reducing our numbers. The task our Queen has given you will determine whether we survive. A heavier burden rests on your shoulders, if I may be permitted to say, than even you, Master, are aware of. By building this tower we are committing a blasphemy. This Royal Tower is an affront to AntGod Himself. We must depart, Master, immediately. I sense the approach of The Imperial Guards.'

'We can't go alone, Zekiel. I fear what we'll encounter. What if that bee was an emissary? A scout? What if we're faced with others of his kind? Or if the knowledge he'd garnered has spread to other species?'

Adam and Zekiel each chose fifty JourneyAnts. By prior arrangement, they had decided on those who had served for some time as both labourers and light infantry. These JourneyAnts, despite having sabre mandibles, large claws, body armour bristling with stiff spikes and peculiarly large bellies gorged with formic acid that could immobilise any hostile bee or spider, were able to move quickly and nimbly in the field of combat. They would present a formidable defensive force against any unexpected foe. For food, Adam took a small herd of greenflies, whose abdomen, once caressed, produced honeydew.

They exited the secret passage several hundred antbody lengths from The Imperial Gate. What greeted them had them freeze in horror. They stood in silence for a long time, watching as thousands of ants began working under moonlight constructing what Adam and Zekiel knew to be the foundations of The Royal Tower.

'My AntGod! Already? So quickly? Work has begun. We're engaged in a race, Zekiel. One we can't win!'

Silence.

'Zekiel? Speak to me! What if the Queen is powerless to stop the construction? By the time we return, will it be too late? Will The Royal Tower be complete?'

'I fear it, Master. I fear him. You know of whom I speak.'

'Those workers, Zekiel, look at them. He's recruited from our young.'

'He has, Master.'

What puzzled Adam was their size.

'They are,' said Zekiel, 'a tenth of the average length of an ant their age. We are in crisis, Master. Our young are shrinking in size. As our population increases, we are producing smaller ants. Any *thereafter* we experience will be barely a thereupon.'

Chapter 6

The Journey to Knowledge

Adam Ant fell back on his rear legs, his entire body emitting pheromones of deep sadness. The progress made by the ants labouring on the foundations was proceeding apace before his very eyes, their enthusiasm, detected even from a distance, plunging him into despair.

'You have authority, Master. You must remain hopeful.'

'But the Queen has given me a task which can't be fulfilled in a brief period, Zekiel! Look at the distance between us and The Sacred Circle of Cliffs. And listen. Can you hear? Those workers are scraping their legs on their bodies, singing in unison and joy as they go about their work. The signs of imminent catastrophe are there for all to see, and they sing? AyJay Heartland has at his disposal millions of ants who'll willingly do his bidding. By the time my task is done he'll be well on the way to completing this tower. And who is there to stand in his way?'

Zekiel draped one of his antennae over Adam. Adam responded. Their antennae touched then interlaced, as they had once before, Zekiel's antenna communicating a sense of warmth, succour and inspiration.

'You say I have authority, Zekiel. What can I achieve alone?'

'Do you believe, Master, in the establishment of a colony?'

'Yes, I do.'

'And do you believe that the construction of The Royal Tower is an affront? To AntGod?'

'Yes, Zekiel, I do.'

'If you have the authority of conviction, Master, of faith that what you are about to do, you do for the common good, that suffices. That is reason enough. Think upon that. The establishment of a new colony will make this abomination that AyJay Heartland is building an irrelevancy. You must remain hopeful, Master, that The Royal Tower will remain empty while any new colony will thrive. Let us focus on what lies ahead. Ahh, look, Master, is it not wondrous?'

Adam and Zekiel gazed in awe at the distant circle of mountains that stood aloof and all-embracing, as if what they looked upon were the arms of AntGod Himself protecting his devotees.

'How peculiar, Zekiel, that beyond such a thing of beauty lies the horror of The NoWorld.'

Zekiel did not respond.

Adam wondered about the nature – the *substance* – of The NoWorld beyond. He was curious, was he not, to ascend. No, he would *not* climb the cliff face. Why would he risk provoking AntGod's anger by attempting to climb any part of The Sacred Circle?

Everyone knew, Adam thought, that such an act would precipitate divine fury ... but why? It had been repeatedly stated as an article of faith, AntGod's will and commandment made manifest.

'Zekiel, where is it written that we're not to step foot on The Sacred Circle?'

'It is not written, Master.'

'Nowhere?'

'Nowhere.'

'Then on whose authority has this commandment been made?'

'I cannot answer, Master.'

'Because? Zekiel, what are you implying?'

'We must keep such thoughts to ourselves, Master.'

'But the answer to my question, Zekiel?'

'There is a truth greater than truth itself, Master.'

'You must speak plainly, Zekiel! You can't answer, or you choose not to answer?'

'Both, Master.'

'You speak in riddles again. We'll talk of this later. Come. We go. First we inspect The Royal Forest.'

To ensure they did not get lost they immediately began counting their steps to determine where they were in relation to the metropolis. They also left scent trails from their dufour glands to point the way to those who would follow them to the site of the new colony once its location had been determined. Such a detailed survey, inscribed in their heads, would also assist Adam and his ants in tracing their way home.

Prior to departing for the forest, Adam did as Zekiel

suggested and inspected the leaves of bushes they harvested to produce the fungi for their larvae. In the few months since Adam had made his most recent inspection, some of the bushes had died.

'Zekiel, you knew they'd perished?'

'I knew.'

'But ... but why hadn't you reported it?'

'I had, Master.'

'And?'

'May I suggest we fulfil the Queen's instruction and inspect our disposal sites?'

They saw the bubbling emission of tiny, smouldering clouds of warm gas.

'This is strange, Zekiel. It's almost as warm outside the city as it is inside!'

'Almost, Master?'

Adam moistened both antennae then scanned the air. He used his elbow brush to dry his antennae then conducted another olfactory test. 'There's no doubt. The odour within the city is the same as that which is being emitted from our waste dumps and our fungus farms. Zekiel? You're not responding. You're not surprised?'

'No.'

'Because you knew.'

'Yes.'

'And you no doubt had reported this, also.'

'Yes, Master.'

'Zekiel, we must head quickly for The Royal Forest. From now on you are responsible for conducting a regular headcount of our JourneyAnts. Conduct one immediately. Once you are done, we leave.'

Zekiel did as Adam had instructed. 'Master, we have a problem.'

'What is it, Zekiel?'

'How many had you chosen for this expedition?'

'Fifty. As had you. Why?'

'Have you inspected them, Master?'

'No. Why do you ask?'

'We have 101 JourneyAnts.'

Adam approached his fellow AntLanders who, awaiting instructions, stood in serried rows. Adam saw one ant standing in the centre column, making small his body so that he would not be spied. Adam pointed him out to Zekiel. 'Did you choose him, Zekiel?'

'No, Master, I had assumed you had chosen him. Do you think AyJay Heartland has sent him as a spy?'

'No, Zekiel, the ChairAnt would not leave himself open to discovery by means of a simple headcount. And this is no ordinary ant. He is certainly not one to betray me.'

'You know him?'

Adam summoned the ant. 'Young Nano, why am I not surprised?'

'I mean well, Master.'

'That is neither here nor there, Nano!'

'It is important that I follow you, Master.'

'That is not for you to decide. You were not chosen by either Zekiel the Wise or myself to accompany us."

'No, Master.'

'You took it upon yourself to join us. You did not ask permission. You spoke to no-one.'

'That is correct, Master.'

'What do you mean by saying that you mean well? Why is it important that you follow me? Important for whom? Me, or yourself? Speak, Nano. Why are you here?'

'I was watching, Master.'

'Watching?' Adam turned to Zekiel. 'I see we have with us an ant that could be your protégé. You're not the only one who speaks in riddles, Zekiel.' He turned back to Nano. "Watching who? Watching what? Watching when? Explain yourself.'

'When our Queen gave her address, I was in The Grand Hall, three rows from the platform.'

'Yes, I saw you.'

'From my position I could see. I was watching.'

'We were all watching. It was, after all, an historical occasion. What has that got to do with you taking it upon yourself to join us?'

'No, Master, I mean, I was watching *you*.'

'I don't understand.'

'I know that AntLand is suffering. I do not know how I know, but I feel AntLand's distress. I have prayed to AntGod to alert us to the cause of the strangeness infecting our empire, to reveal to us what it is that disturbs me, and so I knew that when Her Majesty informed us of your mission, I felt that she was talking to all of us, yes, but also directly to me, and that I had to join you, to help you. My prayers have been answered. You are doing AntGod's work, Master Adam.'

'You said you'd been watching me.'

'I was watching the ChairAnt. I was watching Her Majesty. I felt what passed between you and AyJay Heartland. It was when I was watching you that I understood what was at stake. I want to be with you. You are in danger, Master. I want to help you. I want to protect you. I want to help AntLand. I feel that it is my calling.'

'I suspect you are an ant who will give me heartache, Young Nano.'

'I understand, Master.'

'You understand? Take care, Young Nano. You are being impertinent. How can you know such a thing?'

'Forgive me. I mean no disrespect. I understand why you say such a thing, because I give myself heartache, Master.'

After many weeks travelling they arrived at where they thought The Royal Forest should be. The peculiarity of the landscape did not register on Adam's olfactory map ... nor on any map of his JourneyAnts. They all assumed, therefore, that they must have lost their way. They returned some of the way they had come, calculated again the angle of the sun's rays, double-checked the trails of pheromones and took a variety of routes only to discover that each led to the same area.

Some of the ants wondered whether the heat had affected their sense of direction, but Adam dismissed this. He checked ant droppings and the scents on rocks on the ground. He took his bearings once more from the sun and the forest's distance from The Sacred Circle of Cliffs and compared them to the map in his head. There was no doubt they had stopped in what was once The Royal Forest, but the change was so dramatic as to make it unrecognisable. What to tell his JourneyAnts? The news would break their hearts. This forest had once been thickly wooded. Here were the grandest trees in The Eternal Valley, some reaching dizzying heights. All had been planted by Elders long ago, some to commemorate important occasions such as the fiftieth anniversary of the empire's founding. It was a sacred site, one allowed visitation by subjects during ceremonial occasions only so honoured by Royal Decree. Most of the trees had dried in the heat, their brittle, skeletal stalks stripped of every leaf, their taut branches stretched wide like the extended legs of a long dead monster. A few trees, each no more than twenty antlengths high, struggled to survive. They stood isolated, large patches of barren soil between them. Such were the remnants of a once great forest. Adam gave the order to shift their camp. It was not just because of the lack of shade in the rising temperature: the loathsome odour that had repulsed him in the fungus farms and the disposal site was almost as acute here, in the open.

'How, Zekiel, am I going to tell my JourneyAnts that this is what is left of The Royal Forest?'

'There are those who govern us, Master, who make of their every word an untruth. You are not of that kind. The truth, Master Adam, is that henceforth the wild flowering shrubs of The Royal Forest, its imposing grave trees, its abundance of insect life in and amongst the roots and the leaves and the branches could well become, in time, nothing more than a ghostly memory.'

'No!'

'Yes, Master.'

'It cannot be.'

'I say again: it could well be.'

Once they had established a new camp, Adam thought again of assembling his JourneyAnts and informing them that what they had just seen was, indeed, what was left of The Royal Forest, and that, in time, this ancient site, cherished by generations of subjects, could quite possibly be gone. He imagined some beating their thoraxes with their feet, others falling to the ground and letting out a squealing howl, all praying to AntGod that their sacred site be restored to its former glory.

'Did you notice, Master,' said Zekiel, 'that there are no birds in what is left of the forest?'

'I did.'

'And did you notice, Master, how dry the soil is?'

'Yes, Zekiel.'

Young Nano detected their exchange. He approached and entwined antennae with Adam. 'This is no fable,' he said.

I can't tell them, thought Adam. I won't tell them.

That night, contrary to what Adam predicted, they suffered a terrible, sudden storm. It came upon them so quickly that they were caught unprepared and had to cross raging rivers and avoid falling branches, rescue repeatedly fellow ants who were washed away in sudden torrents and, once they found a hollow tree, one they were obliged to share with many snails, cling to each other to ward off the cold. The cold? Adam's predictions of the weather had always been unfailingly accurate. How could he have been so mistaken?

They smeared themselves and their herd of greenflies with the slime of one of the snails to defend themselves against the bitter storm.

'Master,' Zekiel said, once they had settled for the night, 'do you think the forest can be rehabilitated?'

'Eventually, yes, I do.'

'As do I,' Zekiel said. 'Forgive me, Master, but the truth should not be allowed to the privileged few. Our JourneyAnts deserve to know what we know. Tell them and give them hope.'

And so, Adam gathered his JourneyAnts around him and informed them that what they had seen was, indeed, their cherished Royal Forest. As expected, many became distraught. Adam waited until they had composed themselves. 'There will, however, come a day when it will be restored. I believe this, even if it will not be in our lifetime. It's what I want you to imagine. It's what I choose to believe. Look upon the forest not as what it is, but what it will one day become. Each night I make my petition to AntGod for the good health of our Queen, for our empire to thrive and for us to enjoy a good life. Join me now before we sleep as I make my entreaty, asking also for the rehabilitation of our Royal Forest. Above all, have faith in restoration. I choose faith.'

Adam awoke during the night. He looked across at Nano, who, he saw, was sleeping with his claw against his face in the manner of a recently-born or, he thought, wise old ant: another Zekiel in the making, perhaps? Adam was moved by the affection he felt for this young ant.

As if sensing Adam's feelings, Nano opened his eyes. 'Did we also choose AntGod, Master?'

Adam rested an antenna on Nano's head. 'Sleep,' he said.

'What is a good life, Master Adam?'

'We have a long journey ahead of us.' How, Adam wondered, was it possible for so young a body to have so old a head? 'We can talk of such matters later. You'll need your energy tomorrow, Nano.' He left his antenna resting on Nano and watched as the young ant attempted, with little success, to return to sleep.

'Master Adam?'

'Yes, Nano?'

'Zekiel is old.'

'Yes, he is. That was not a question, Nano. Why do you say what is obvious?'

'I was wondering, Master, if, because you have so many worries, you had not noticed.'

'That he is old?'

'No, Master, that he struggles at times to keep up with us.'

'Ah, Nano, I'm ashamed to say I had not noticed.'

'You have much on your mind, Master.'

The following morning the sun rose on a clear day. Adam's JourneyAnts were pleased, but he was perplexed. He searched the air and took a reading of the elements. He had predicted it would rain. Once again, he was wrong. It was a day of unrelenting heat, so intense that they could only cover half the ground that they had intended to explore. Adam had them take refuge in a crevice in which, by sheer good fortune, they came across a large earwig that was so preoccupied eating dead insect remains that it noticed none of the AntLanders. Adam sprang into action. Folding back the part of his abdomen behind his thorax and propping himself on his rear legs, he propelled a stream of formic acid into the earwig's eyes. The JourneyAnts immediately fell upon the creature, dispatching it with their own supply of formic acid.

They feasted that night on this earwig, their dwindling supply of fructose, honeydew from their greenflies and the remains of a number of caterpillars that had died long ago and had dried in the sun, burrowing into what was left of hollowed-out bodies to escape another storm.

The next day Adam conducted another reading. His confidence, however, had been shaken by his prior incorrect predictions, and so he decided not to inform his JourneyAnts that his senses indicated the day would be hot and dry. His hesitancy was well founded. By midday the sky began to quickly darken. A whistling breeze was the sign for Adam that they should seek shelter. He led his ants across a featureless stretch of dry ground on which they were buffeted by mighty winds. The temperature dropped dramatically. Thunder rolled across a blackening sky moments after he had come across a long-disused spider's hole in which they found protection from hail as big as their heads. They stood as one at the opening and watched in awe as mighty pieces of ice fell crashing to the ground. The roar of the storm was something none of them had ever experienced. Long after they had settled, a few of the ants approached Adam and asked him what he thought the next day's weather would be. He had little confidence the prediction he made would come to pass.

In the two months that followed the hailstorm, they were blessed with weather which, while unpredictable, allowed them time to explore. They mapped out slightly less than half of the plains. While his ants surveyed sites for a colony, he searched for the trees that supplied the empire with compost leaves. AntLand's one source of compost, he discovered, had become scarce.

And predicting the weather had become pointless. This was clear the longer they travelled: heat spells were followed by a dramatic fall in temperature and wild storms preceded periods of calm. They lost over half their herd of greenflies during one of the most violent storms they encountered. Instability, Adam realised, was becoming the norm. AntGod was, indeed, reacting adversely to the construction of The Royal Tower.

On his return, would he alert his fellow AntLanders as to what he knew? Such knowledge would create panic in the empire. But how could he keep such a thing to himself? Who to tell that something bizarre had taken a firm grip on The Eternal Valley?

Only one: the Queen.

Three months into the expedition, Adam realised he had no choice: he had to cut short his mission and return to the metropolis as a matter of extreme urgency. Just over half of The Eternal Valley had been explored and still no site had been found for the colony. But the increasing frequency of extreme weather, the destruction of The Royal Forest and the inevitable collapse of their source of leaves for their fungi farms required the empire's immediate attention. Some of the Elders would, no doubt, query his findings, particularly those who were unquestioning supporters of AyJay Heartland, but he had Zekiel and his 101 JourneyAnts to verify what he had discovered.

Adam decided to inform his team of his decision once they reached The Queen's Lake, a large body of water that lay within one day's walk of The Sacred Circle of Cliffs. As soon as they arrived, he ordered them to build a camp near the water's edge: they would rest for one day and night beside the lake before beginning the long journey back to the metropolis. After giving his instructions, he set off with Zekiel and Nano to explore the lake.

While walking, Adam told Zekiel of his plan to return to the metropolis. 'You have done well, Zekiel, to keep up with us. I thank you, too, for your wise counsel. However, I can return faster if I go ahead of you. It is imperative the Elders are told what we've seen. I shall depart tomorrow.'

'Yes, you must return, and quickly. Take Nano with you, Master. Leave me with but a handful of our JourneyAnts.'

The three arrived at a point directly opposite where the JourneyAnts were setting up their camp. They stopped. They sat. Adam considered the consequences of the irregularity of severe hot and cold spells they had experienced. He had to think about the course of action the empire would be compelled to take to prepare for the day when they might have no leaves to process into compost. He was thinking on these things when he was suddenly seized with fear. Something was wrong. Without moving his antennae, without moving any part of his body, he took a reading of the air.

'Do as I'm doing,' he said to Zekiel and Nano. 'What do you sense?'

It was teeming with toxins, an extreme concentration of the odour Adam had detected on the day of the Queen's address. The intensity of this odour, however, was overpowering. It was dangerous to stay in what he had thought of as an idyllic spot. They had to depart, and quickly.

And then Adam froze. 'There's something else here, a scent on the ground, at my feet, some rank smell that is ... it's familiar and yet ... strange. Do you detect it, Zekiel? Nano?'

Adam slowly lowered one of his antennae. Trembling, he lowered the other. He bent low. Zekiel and Nano were watching Adam scrape the ground with one of his antennae when the Elder involuntarily leapt backwards, away from the trail – because that's what it was, a path comprised of a scent that was the most enticing and repellent smell he had ever detected. Adam approached it again. He lowered both antennae. He sniffed the ground and the air. He absorbed the olfactory message and, fidgeting with his antennae, suddenly knew what he had come upon.

'What, Master? What is it?' cried Zekiel.

'It's the pheromones of an ant, a single ant, but ... but not one of our kind.'

'An alien?'

Here Adam stood, confirming with his antennae over and over and over again the extraordinary discovery he had made: an ant not of their species. What did this mean? That there was antlife outside AntLand? Of course that is what it meant. So he, his JourneyAnts, The Queen, AyJay Heartland, The Council of Elders, the thirty million subjects of the empire, were not alone in the universe? If his repeated readings were correct – and he knew they were, try as hard as he could to dismiss them – then here was the evidence, here was the proof of ...

He shuddered to consider the implications of what he had discovered: for where there was one alien ant there would be many – perhaps friend, perhaps foe.

Was it fearless recklessness, a yearning to know, a longing to make contact with life beyond the known world, or a desire to protect the empire? Adam Ant did not know. But he would find out. He would take Zekiel with him and follow this trail to see where it might lead.

'Nano, return to the camp. Stay with the others.'

Chapter 7

Contact Made with an Alien

The alien pheromones led them away from the lake towards the cliffs. It was late in the afternoon. Adam could not stay out alone with Zekiel once night fell. Who knew what dangers this alien represented? Nor could he risk the possibility of this trail being corrupted at night by some urinating reptile or washed away by a violent storm. He had made a discovery that would shatter so much of what his fellow AntLanders believed. There was no choice. He and Zekiel had to exercise caution and return alive to the empire with the extraordinary news that they were not the only ants in AntGod's kingdom, that within the confines of The Sacred Circle of Cliffs there lived another species of ant and that ... But what if they did *not* inhabit The Eternal Valley? What if ...

And at that moment Adam Ant knew he was considering what had previously been unthinkable, sacrilegious – dare he use the word – *blasphemous*. What if these aliens did not reside in the valley but inhabited The NoWorld, what AntLanders had always been told was The Great Darkness?

Adam looked back at his fellow AntLanders. He saw them reclining on the banks of the lake, no doubt exhausted from the 100 odd days during which they had battled heatwaves, rugged terrain and thunderous storms of wind, rain and hail. They had disobeyed him by not completing their setting-up of the camp. This was the first occasion they had not followed his command. Adam held his breath – the toxicity of the odour was particularly acute – and observed his fellow JourneyAnts lying together in a tight huddle. They had been loyal followers. Perhaps I have pushed them too hard, he thought. The Elder felt a wave of compassion overwhelm him, knowing that he might not return from what he was about to embark upon. He should, he knew, take a few AntLanders with him. But he was reluctant to disturb their peace, place them once again in a situation that threatened their lives. Besides, time was of the essence: the sun was sinking fast.

He could now perceive the noxious smell as low-lying, motionless clouds, floating close to the surface of the lake and reflecting the glow of the setting sun. How deceptive things could be, he thought. The odorous patches of fog were lovely to look upon but surely harmful to inhale. The variegated orange glowing bands, that were such a contrast to the acrid, pervasive smell, could, he thought, be the last object of beauty they set eyes on; the alien ant could be close by, watching, waiting in ambush.

They extended their antennae to pursue the alien's scent, tracking the trail with small, carefully-placed uniform treads, all the while scrutinising the orientation of the land upon which they walked and the cliff face towards which they knew they were being led. Adam need not have concerned himself at losing the smell: so powerful was it, far more than that emitted by AntLanders, that he was able to attend it with ease, even when the trail led to a marshy bog. Adam and Zekiel leapt from grass blade to grass blade and pebble to pebble, Zekiel stumbling at times but brushing aside Adam's concerns. They swam across puddles, some as wide as ten antbody lengths, and stepped lightly through mud, focusing so intently on the lie of the land, the caustic smell of the pheromones and the looming cliffs that they almost fell into a fast-flowing stream. Adam had paused by its bank to take stock of his surroundings when he noticed something else that was peculiar. He followed with his eyes the course of this stream to where it began.

Zekiel interrupted his thoughts. 'Its source is the snow melting on the summit of the cliffs, Master.'

It was not so much its origin, however, that intrigued Adam, or the fact that it poured down the side of the cliff face with such great speed. The stream gushed past him only to disappear into a chasm. Was there a great lake beneath the surface of The Eternal Valley? He dipped a mandible into the cold water. He tasted it. It was unlike anything he had ever tasted: refreshingly pure, unusually sweet and invigorating.

As Adam expected, their pursuit of the trail led directly to The Sacred Circle of Cliffs. This was where his trailing of the alien should have ended. It was, after all, one of the most sacred of AntLand's commandments that no ant set foot upon the cliff where, it was said, AntGod Himself resided. Should anyone step on this Holy of Holies, one was immediately struck down.

'Said by whom, Zekiel?'

'The one who has most to gain, Master; you know of whom I speak.'

Perhaps Adam would, at that moment, have turned back to join his fellow ants. Perhaps he would have done what his aching logic told him: return to the metropolis, seek – no, demand – an audience with the Queen, tell her all he had discovered, if Zekiel had not spied a movement, a flash of colour, the smell of pheromones so distinct that he knew, he knew with absolute certainty, that the alien was alone and was close to where they stood.

'There he is is, Master!' He pointed. 'To your left! There! There! He's only a few antbody lengths away.'

Adam had already taken a mighty leap, landing on a rock on the cliff face. He stood on the rock, eyes tightly shut, antennae held stiff and still, fearing that every moment might be his last. He opened them to find Zekiel at his side. Still shaking with fear, Adam looked up at The Sacred Circle of Cliffs. But all he saw were the glorious rays of the setting sun reflecting off its snow-capped peaks. He noticed droplets breaking free from the fall of water, sparkling and singing as they made their dramatic descent; saw, too, a glistening stream pouring off an overhanging shelf then falling through moist clouds of vapour. He followed the glorious torrent cascading down the mountainside and landing with a thud on the water drummed earth. And that was when he and Zekiel saw a long, slender, yellow ant with the dismembered leg of a lizard in its huge mandibles and the hooked claws of its two front legs holding down its writhing victim, watching them. Adam was so startled that he fell off the rock and tumbled backwards and downwards. During his descent he saw the alien drop the severed lizard's limb and scramble up the mountainside towards the summit of the cliff. Zekiel rushed in his old ant fashion to Adam's aid.

Adam, terrified, rose to his feet before Zekiel arrived and ran as fast as he could towards The Queen's Lake, falling, in his haste, into the stream and managing – with the assistance of Nano – to escape the flood of water pouring into the chasm.

'Nano! What are you doing here? I told you ——'

Zekiel called out. 'Wait, Master!'

Adam and Nano clambered up the bank, slipping and sliding repeatedly until they were on firm soil. They ran like they were being pursued by a starving beast, Adam marvelling that he had the presence of mind to not only detect the merging of his trail of pheromones with that of the bizarrely-coloured alien, but also to notice Zekiel fall and clumsily rise to his feet before lumbering after them.

When they were 200 or so antbody lengths away from the cliff, Adam stopped, every nerve in his body tingling, his breathing wild and erratic, and turned to see if they had been followed by the alien. They had not. What Adam did see, however, was the yellow ant perched on a ledge, watching them, his antennae jerking this way and that. The alien began licking his antennae to dampen them, after which he stroked one antenna then the other with his elbow brush, turned and resumed his long, slow ascent to the top of the cliff, finally disappearing amongst some boulders.

Zekiel finally caught up with Adam and Nano.

'What was that, Zekiel?'

'Master, a more pertinent question would be: *Do you know what this means?*'

'And as for you, Nano, you disobeyed me,' said Adam. 'I told you to join my JourneyAnts.'

'I was afraid for you. Forgive me, Master. I meant well. I have my pledge to uphold.'

'I don't want to keep hearing you say you mean well when you disobey me. You must do as you're told, Nano. Do you understand? And pledge. What pledge? To whom have you made a pledge?"

"To myself, Master. To protect you.'

'You exasperate me, Nano.'

'I exasperate myself, Master.'

'Did you see what we saw?'

'Yes, Master.'

'What did you see, Nano?'

'A yellow ant, Master. An alien.'

They walked slowly to The Queen's Lake, in deep conflict over what to do.

'Nano, walk twenty paces behind us.'

Adam waited until Nano was out of hearing range. 'Zekiel? I'm ... I don't know what to say, what to think.'

'I believe you do know, Master. I surmise that you do not want to believe what you know to be true.'

'You saw it first, Zekiel.'

'Yes.'

'You warned me, but your warning came too late to prevent me from leaping onto the cliff face.'

'Yes, Master.'

'Onto the *sacred* cliff face, Zekiel.'

'Please Master, speak your mind.'

'I acted impulsively, Zekiel, leapt when a part of me knew it was an act of madness. But you? You followed me. After all that we've been told as to what would happen to us should we climb this ... this holy site, you – who could have stayed where you were – came after me, with no delay. Why?'

'It is my role, Master, to ensure your wellbeing, to do whatever I can to have you return to our metropolis. I, too, have made a pledge, to our Queen, no less.'

Adam was silent. He scanned Zekiel with his antennae. He stepped back, thinking, watching this old sage. 'There's more, Zekiel. You're keeping some thoughts to yourself. Speak.'

'There are some notions one cannot discuss easily, Master.'

'I await your sharing of those notions, Zekiel the Wise.'

Zekiel did not speak.

'Then allow me to begin for you,' said Adam. 'You came after me because you knew both you and I weren't in danger. I refer to AntGod, Zekiel, not that creature we saw. You knew there'd be no retribution once we landed on the Sacred Circle of Cliffs. Am I correct?'

'There are some notions ...'

'No! I want an answer. And I want it now.'

'The answer to your question is, yes, I knew there would be no divine punishment, not for you, not for me.'

Adam turned to ensure Nano was well behind him. 'You don't believe in AntGod?'

'Oh, I believe, Master, of that I have no doubt. But we are not designed to hold a firm grasp of intricacies. Certainty in specifics is not in our charter.'

'Zekiel! Plain speaking, please!'

'You ask for what I cannot give. Allow me to convey my paltry knowledge. No, not knowledge, but understanding. Allow me, then, to communicate what I believe, in the following manner: we ants have a sense of what lies beyond, but that is what it can only ever be. It is our limitation that gives rise to delineations.'

'Such as what AntGod demands of us?'

'Such as specific laws whose origins are antmade.'

'Such as,' Adam said, 'prohibitions regarding setting foot on The Sacred Circle of Cliffs?'

'Yes.'

'And now? What now, Zekiel? Return immediately to AntLand and tell all of what we've done and seen? Of what we *sense*? Would I not risk undermining my authority and risk losing my position as an Elder by informing them, or anybody for that matter, that I've set foot on The Sacred Circle?'

'You would not *risk* it, Master. You would *lose* it. There are few matters in this antworld of ours that are certain. That is one of them.'

'And as for telling them of the alien, they'll think I'm either a liar or an ant who's lost his mind.'

'Yes. AyJay will say you are both a blasphemer and a mad-ant.'

'But how can I not tell?'

'You cannot keep such knowledge to yourself, Master.'

Adam, Zekiel and Nano entered the camp. They found all 100 JourneyAnts lying in a heap, dead.

Chapter 8

Adam, Zekiel and Nano
Bear Witness to The NoWorld

Adam knew immediately what had occurred. AntGod had not struck him down but had, instead, chosen to punish him by having those for whom he was responsible die an appalling death, knowing that the guilt would plague him for the rest of his life. His AntLanders lay in all manner of contortions encased, as if still alive, in their gleaming exoskeletons, their mouths agape, their soft tissue, Adam could see, contracted into withered strands and lumps and a harrowing look of terror in their eyes. They died knowing, Adam thought with horror, of their impending death.

'What have I done, Zekiel? It's clear, isn't it, that I have angered AntGod?'

Adam and Nano were exhausted. Zekiel had fared worse; oftentimes he walked unsteadily, his antennae trembling, his worn and battered legs occasionally causing him to trip and fall. Adam knew that the three of them were in imminent danger. The alien could return and, for a few weary moments, Adam told himself that he did not care. He would accept death were it to come that moment, that hour or that night. He lay down beside his dead AntLanders and stared out onto the lake, the light of a half-moon glimmering on its surface.

'No, Master, it is not in AntGod's nature to punish others for our sins. And we must never assume to know the mind of AntGod.'

'Do you believe that, Zekiel, or are you just trying to comfort me?'

'I would never lie to you, Master.'

'*Ahhh*, forgive me, Zekiel.'

Adam watched as the moon's glow revealed the shapes of the low-lying odorous clouds. A light breeze had them drift slowly towards him. Strange, it was, that in all that had happened he had forgotten his previous decision to lead his charges away from these pungent, acidic smells. It was now too late. The clouds, suffused with all sorts of strange colours, floated onto the water itself ... or, at least, seemed to.

Adam raised his head. He took note of the peculiar behaviour of the gaseous vapour. He sat up. He watched. He saw an enormous bubble rise from the depths of the lake only to suddenly burst. The heavy cloud emitted by this explosion stalked the banks opposite to where he sat. He saw a grasshopper and several frogs by the side of the lake, in the direct path of the gas. One by one each creature collapsed, twisting and squirming in acute pain until it expired, mouth open and eyes full of horror. He looked at his AntLanders. He saw the same features on their faces.

No, it had *not* been AntGod who had taken the lives of his workers! The gas he had detected the day of the Queen's address, the odour he and his AntLanders had had to contend with every day of their journey, was becoming more poisonous with the passing of time, and here, here in the bodies of his JourneyAnts, was the evidence.

Adam rose to his feet. 'Zekiel? Do you see what I see?'

'Yes, Master.'

The breeze shifted. The deadly fog changed direction. More bubbles burped their clouds into the air. Adam could feel and taste the bitter, toxic poison burning his mouth, the insides of his abdomen, felt himself become dizzy and nauseous. They had to flee this terrible place; its beauty was a trap. 'Run!'

Zekiel found a small hollow in the log of a tree that had fallen generations ago. He, Nano and Adam snuggled as far as they could into its depths, hoping they would survive the night. Adam did not pray. He would not pray. He and Zekiel had set foot on the holy mount and had not been struck down. They had seen the alien ant climb towards the top of the cliff and not be struck down. Was AntGod a myth? But created by whom?

He considered the river flowing incessantly into that chasm and recalled the waterlogged lower depths of the metropolis he had accidentally wandered into not long before the Queen gave her speech. He remembered the water dripping from many unseen sources and the complete absence of pheromones in those lower chambers, a clear indication that those sections of AntLand had been abandoned long ago. Was it possible that the water falling from the peaks of the cliffs was flowing through some underground tunnel and emerging in the metropolis itself? Could this vast body of water completely overwhelm an entire metropolis?

And was there some way the odour he had detected in the metropolis was finding its way through that same underground tunnel and emerging here, near the base of The Sacred Circle of Cliffs? Or was it the other way around: that these odours originated here, at this lake? And if these deadly gases, these noxious clouds that had infiltrated AntLand – whatever their source: perhaps from the vents of the metropolis? was that possible? – became as intense and as toxic as those that had killed his followers, then there was nothing to prevent them from floating through tunnel after tunnel, percolating into every room and chamber of the metropolis, wreaking havoc in the empire, seeping even into The Royal Chamber itself.

And what of that long-legged yellow ant, who now knew of Adam and Zekiel and possibly Nano too? This alien would return to his own queen and inform her of the black ants he had seen in the valley. And then what?

That night, a wild storm struck terror in his heart. But, on emerging the following morning from their sanctuary, Adam saw no vaporous clouds, no evidence of a toxic fog and no stealthy gases. The winds of the previous night had, he thought, dissipated those odours that had taken the lives of his 100 followers. He, Zekiel and Nano, he knew, had to flee the scene to return as quickly as possible to AntLand.

They walked for five days and nights, using the sun as a lodestar during the day, while at night they retraced their steps, swinging their antennae from side to side to pick up the odours they had previously created. All three punished themselves so that Adam could, upon their return, deliver the news of the terrible threats facing the empire. They slept rarely, Zekiel denying himself the rest breaks his aching, ageing body needed. They suffered heat waves and cold snaps, floods and storms. They were even attacked by caterpillars that AntLand had long ago assumed were tamed.

'The old world is changing, Zekiel.'

The old ant did not reply.

'Zekiel the Wise, I need to hear you speak.'

Zekiel made a sound of solicitude.

'I have long respected your solemn composure, Zekiel, your austere self-possession. Now is not the time to be reserved. Have you nothing to say to give me hope?'

'You told me once that you held my silences in great esteem, Master. There are occasions when words do not suffice.'

'No! No, no, no! How can you not speak when you're able to recall what we had once? When you know what it is that we have lost? The Royal Forest. Days, weeks, months of predictable weather. The orderly maintenance of our crops and livestock.'

Zekiel received Adam's rebuke standing sombre and still. 'Yes.'

'Yes? Is that all you have to say?'

'I remember, Master,' Zekiel said, without that quiet authority that Adam had long taken for granted.

'Speak up, Zekiel. I can barely hear you.'

'I remember, Master, the clear mornings.'

'Yes, yes, go on!'

'I remember the welcome and expected change of the seasons,' he said, his voice flat and grave. 'Each with its bounty. Yes, and so. The life-giving rains. The life-giving sun. The rich smell of the soil. The sudden growth after the AntGod-bestowed gifts. Gifts of sun and light and rain. The vigour and youthfulness and brightness of the unspoilt morning. Every day presenting us with that great bowl of The Eternal Plain over which we roamed, harvesting with ease all that we required for those whom we fed. I remember when I would inhale the freshness of the air. I would thank AntGod for such an offering. As I would for thunder. And lightning. Seeing them as evidence of AntGod's benefaction.' He paused. He waited, proud and upright and tired and very, very old. 'And now that I have given Master what he asked for, and what I regret Nano had to hear, I shall be silent.'

Adam, unable to sleep that night, stirred Zekiel. 'Are you awake?'

'Yes, Master.'

'Forgive me, Zekiel. I spoke harshly to you. My transgression has made me ill. I'm sick with remorse.'

'Yes, I know, Master.'

'Zekiel?'

'Yes, Master?'

'When I asked you to speak, when I insisted you speak, I asked that you give me hope.'

'Yes, you did.'

'But you gave me none.'

'No, I did not.'

'Why, Zekiel?'

'I am afraid, Master.'

'As am I. There's something else I want to ask you, Zekiel.'

'I feel the fear in your voice, Master.'

'I'm afraid of your response to what I'm going to ask.'

'Must you ask it?'

'Yes, I must.'

'What is your question, Master?'

'Prior to our Queen landing for the first time in The Eternal Valley, she had to have come from somewhere, some other nest, yes?'

Silence.

'She had to have been inseminated by an ant, otherwise how could she have given birth to the subject-ants of AntLand – to you, to me, to Nano? To all of us?'

Silence.

'How did this myth originate, that we are the masters of the universe? How many ant-nests do you think are out there? Zekiel? You have nothing to say?'

'Hush. These are not thoughts for Nano to hear.'

Adam turned to Nano. 'Nano, are you awake?'

Nano raised his head. 'Yes, Master.'

They were about to set off when Zekiel, the first to awaken, ran both antennae on the ground, searched the air then, standing erect, cried out aloud. 'He was here! Last night. The alien, Master, was here. Wake up! Nano, get up.' It was, Zekiel told them, a trail that was so powerful it could only have been produced with the express purpose of it being discovered. 'This yellow ant is no threat, Master. I feel it. I sense it. He could have killed us during the night. The alien has searched for us and, finding us, left his pheromones. His pheromones are a summons.'

'A summons? Who's being summoned?'

'We are.'

'But why behave so surreptitiously?" asked Adam. 'Why not make his intentions known, make a more direct contact?'

'Perhaps,' said Nano, 'he is afraid of *us*.'

'Yes!' said Zekiel. 'Yes, Nano, you echo my thoughts. You must trust me, Master. I know what we must do. There can be no other explanation. Why? Why come all this way if not for that? What other explanation can there be? We were vulnerable last night, Master. We were at his mercy while we were asleep. And what does he do? Leave this trail that is so powerful we could not possibly have not detected it.'

They set off after the trail, apprehensive and excited. They were two days from The Queen's Lake, retracing their steps, when the breeze that had been offering them some relief suddenly turned violent, giving them no time to prepare for the swirling, haphazard assault of a suffocating dust storm that, in a few moments, reduced visibility to one antbody. Fine particles of dirt covered their antennae, playing havoc with their sense of direction. They had to cling to thick, fallen branches lest the wind scatter them into the strange, whirling cloud that made breathing difficult. Their eyes stung. They gasped for air. They inhaled so much dust that they felt they might choke to death. It was as if they had an intimation of The NoWorld, The Great Darkness beyond The Sacred Circle of Cliffs, a void of confusion in which, it was said, howling, unseen voices and mouths reeking of ghastly odours could ignite their very bodies and have them disintegrate into ash.

They found an escape by chance. Or was it? They detected the pheromones of the alien and followed its trail. It led to a deep hollow in an enormous branch. The alien was not there, but Zekiel was certain it had come to their rescue. They sat out two whole days until the storm blew over, emerging into a still, breathless plain, colourless and dry, to find that the creature had recently, perhaps the previous night, emitted another powerful trail, which they followed.

They paused at The Queen's Lake to give Zekiel the opportunity to gather his strength and to pay homage to the fallen 100, staying well away from the bubbles of gas exploding from the lake. The air, which had become fouler during their eight day absence, was almost as difficult to breathe as when they had been caught in the dust storm. They then returned to the scent, which took them to the base of The Sacred Circle of Cliffs and that fast-flowing stream that had its origins in the snow on the clifftop. The ground was soggy and cold. Adam paused. He made a pact with himself. Should he have any inkling that the alien was not friend but foe – any at all, regardless of how slight the evidence – it was imperative that they flee, that they return to AntLand and, come what may, he had to force his way into the Queen's chamber, or whatever room AyJay Heartland had used to imprison the Queen, and inform her of all that he knew.

He stepped onto the trail the alien had left on the side of the cliff, and waited. AntGod did not send a thunderbolt to destroy him. The ground did not shake. There was no rockslide.

'I've been lied to, Zekiel,' he sighed. 'We've all been lied to.'

They climbed until nightfall then set up camp. The ground was damp – a welcome relief from the heat. They ate some honeydew and slept. All three were certain they were being led to The NoWorld.

They set off early the following morning, estimating it would take the rest of that day to reach the snowline and another to arrive at the clifftop. It was as they had anticipated. On the second day, late in the afternoon, Adam, Zekiel and Nano stood on snow for the first time in their life. It was a thing of great wonder. They retreated to ground more familiar to them to make camp for the night, intending to rise well before dawn the following morning and climb to the summit, thus becoming the first ants in the history of AntLand to gaze upon The NoWorld. They would make the final ascent in the dark so that they would be accompanied by the rising of the sun when they witnessed whatever was on the other side of The Sacred Circle of Cliffs. History dictated that they make of the occasion something significant.

They lay in the dark, unable to sleep.

'Master Adam?'

'Yes, Nano.'

'Who was it who told us that to step onto The Sacred Circle of Cliffs would occasion instant death?'

'Everyone, Nano.'

'Zekiel?'

'Yes, Nano?'

'Earlier today, Master Adam said that we have been lied to. Have we been lied to?'

'It is a myth, Nano.'

'It is not true?'

'It is not,' said Zekiel.

'But is it a lie?'

'It is an untruth, Nano.'

'You do not want to use the word *lie*.'

'Is that a question, Nano?'

'I do not think so. Master Adam?'

'Yes, Nano.'

'Tell me about the founding of AntLand.'

'But you know the story.'

'Tell me.'

'Everyone knows it. Why do you ask?'

'I want to see.'

Adam sat up. He saw the wide-eyed interest in all of Nano's eyes, the query in his upturned face, the sadness in his quivering voice. 'You want to see if I believe it?'

'No. I want to see if you will tell me an untruth.'

'Again, Nano, you exasperate me.'

'I cannot help it, Master. I ——'

'I know. You exasperate yourself. Go to sleep, Nano.'

'Yes, Master.'

One hour later, Nano suddenly broke the silence. 'Would you have told me an untruth, Master?'

'No, Nano, I wouldn't have.'

'Thank you, Master.'

'Go to sleep, Nano.'

'Yes, Master.'

After several minutes, Nano spoke. 'I needed to hear you say that, Master.'

'I understand, Nano.'

They lay stirring in the night. No-one slept.

'Nano?'

'Yes, Master?'

'I needed to hear myself say that.'

'Thank you, Master. In all of AntLand, you and Zekiel are the ones I admire the most.'

'Go to sleep, Nano.'

'I think you are both admirable.'

'Nano, stop talking.'

'Yes, Master.'

They awoke several hours later and set off immediately, aware of the momentousness of what was about to occur. Their reckless bravery in following the trail of the creature into unknown territory and defying ancient AntLand commandments made them heady with excitement and trepidation – a strange combination of fear and enthusiasm. As they scrambled up the incline they felt, at one and the same time, the heat rising from The Eternal Valley and the icy wind blowing across the melting snow buffeting them. They arrived and stood speechless on the windswept top, the light of the moon and many stars glimmering in the snow. They were surprised that the nauseous odour had found its way to these heights.

The sun began its ascent. From where they stood they could see almost the entire Sacred Circle of Cliffs. Adam looked down onto what he had been told was The NoWorld, its vastness making miniscule The Eternal Valley, AntLand a mere pocket in the great lands that stretched almost beyond what eye and antennae could perceive.

The universe was greater than he had ever imagined.

AntLand was not the universe and The NoWorld was not some fearful abyss of darkness and dread.

The NoWorld as it had been described did not exist.

And more: for what was on the floor of the plain appeared to be a moving forest, a body of oddly-coloured vegetation that swayed and shifted. Plant-life that moved? What was this? Adam and Zekiel debated as to what they should do, knowing all the while that they *would* follow the trail of alien pheromones, that they neither could nor should resist the compulsion to follow the yellow ant.

They had been making their way down for most of the morning when the pheromone trail suddenly ended at a ditch. They lay low, puzzled at what they saw below them. They crawled out of the ditch, proceeding with caution, pausing behind various objects so as not to be seen. But not to be seen *by what*? What was that shifting forest? They scuttled from stone to pebble, from branch to grass blade, dragging their bodies low to the ground towards a rock ten times an ant's height that had cracks that allowed them to observe while being themselves unobserved. They lay still, watching.

It was no moving forest. What they looked down upon was a vast area occupied by innumerable settlements of ants, great and small. They saw ants that were much larger than them and others that were so small they could barely be seen. There were ants with long venomous stings and others with mandibles larger than their bodies. Some emerged out of nests under the ground, while others had made their homes on branches of dead trees or inside logs. There were red, yellow and green ants, even ants with a metal lustre. Some appeared to be loners. Others were in groups with a dozen or so members. Some species, though, were highly organised and lived in settlements consisting of thousands of ants. All, however, appeared to be haggard. All appeared to be undernourished, especially the young who were clearly stunted. And there were piles of mummified dead everywhere, too many to count. Adam assumed they had died of starvation.

They remained there for most of the day, Adam collecting information he knew no-one back at AntLand would believe, and were about to depart when they were aghast to see two red ants grasp the extremities of a green ant while a third used its huge mandibles to cut their writhing victim in two.

Adam knew they were in mortal danger. They had to leave before they were seen. Instead they froze. Another sight, one so appalling it could never have been imagined, greeted them. Thousands of large, red ants emerged from the roots of a long-dead tree and marched in strict formation towards a nest of small, green ants. When the smaller ants realised they were under attack, hundreds emerged to defend their homeland, throwing themselves with heroic but useless fervour onto the larger enemy who, with one vicious bite, were able to slice through the head, thorax or abdomen of the defenders. The green ants poured out of the entry of their nest not realising that this attack of the red ants was a ruse: another battalion of the enemy had broken into two columns and, with great precision, had encircled the green ants' city. The red ants waited in formation then began, with formidable military precision, to advance towards the defenders, whom they quickly dispatched. They then poured into the city, emerging holding the eggs of their enemy, immediately sharing the spoils with their fellow ants. The eggs were consumed, right there, on the battlefield.

Adam, Zekiel and Nano were too terrified to move. They

watched, their hearts pounding, as the red ants returned to their nest. The battlefield was littered with dead and dying green ants interspersed with a few red ones. The nest of the green ants had been destroyed. When the last of the red ants had scurried back into their home, ants of several other species appeared from various hideaways. They hesitantly explored the site of the battle then, as one, began rubbing their body parts together. The vibrations created a song. Adam and Zekiel soon realised the ants were mourning their lost loved ones.

They were about to return to the campsite of the previous night when they saw another species of ant, distinguished by its enormous mandibles, surface from a hole in the ground. These ants went from corpse to corpse then, having explored much of the battlefield, began feasting on the dead. Other ants emerged from tree stumps and the roots of dead plants to consume the bodies of the fallen. Some surfaced in large groups, others were clearly solitary.

As they watched, horrified by the widespread cannibalism, a massive swarm of tiny ants suddenly appeared from several exit points in the ground, attacking those who had beaten them to the bodies of the fallen. Everywhere they looked they saw ants bickering over the spoils. Adam was repulsed by the barbarity of the sight and, truth to tell, was comforted as well. Could it be that these ants, enemies of one another, posed no threat to AntLand as long as their enmity was directed towards each other?

As they made their way back to the previous night's campsite, Nano, visibly shaken by what he'd seen, said, 'They ate each other?'

'Are you,' said Adam, 'asking me or telling me?'

'I'm asking. I need to ask.'

'Why?'

'I need to know whether to believe it.'

'You saw it, Nano, as did Zekiel and I. With your own eyes, you saw.'

'I do not believe what I saw. Please answer. They ate each other?'

'Yes, Nano, they ate each other.'

'Master?'

'Yes, Nano?'

'Why are they there?'

'Where?'

'There. There, where they are.'

'I don't know.'

'Do they know AntLand exists?'

'I don't know that, either.'

'Do you think they might have learnt about our reserves of food from the bee that entered our metropolis? The one you killed?'

'I can't answer your questions, Nano.'

'That bee flew into our farmlands, our storerooms, saw our aphids and our caterpillars. Do we know if bees are able to communicate with other species?'

'Please, Nano, you must ——'

'They are starving?'

'Are you asking me or telling me?'

'I am asking, Master.'

'It would appear so. Yes, Nano, they're starving.'

'If they do know of AntLand, will they come for our reserve supplies of food?'

'No ... I don't ... yes, Nano, they will.'

'Will we give them food?'

Adam exchanged a knowing look with Zekiel. 'We should.'

'Yes, we should, but will we?'

Adam thought of AyJay Heartland and the hold he had over The Council of Elders. 'Our Queen would.'

'Would AyJay Heartland?'

'No,' Adam said, 'I don't think he would.'

'And if we do not, what will the aliens do?'

They arrived at their camp to find that the yellow alien had drenched the area with pheromones, leaving them with a greeting, a request and a threat.

They were too agitated to sleep that night.

'Master Adam?'

'Yes, Nano.'

'The silence is terrible.'

'Yes, it is.'

'I cannot sleep.'

'I don't think any of us will be sleeping tonight.'

'Master, I am frightened.'

'Come here.'

Adam entwined antennae with the younger ant and felt the shaking of his body. 'Nano, I can feel your fear in the rise and fall of your breathing.'

'It is your breathing, Master, not mine.'

Later that night, Zekiel reclined beside Adam and Nano. The three of them lay huddled side by side, looking at each other, looking at nothing, thinking.

'Zekiel?'

'Yes, Nano.'

'Are there more of them than us?'

'I do not know, Nano. It is impossible to say. Most of their nests appear to be underground.'

'They are violent.'

'Yes, they are.'

Nano sat up, looking here and there.

'What are you looking at, Nano?'

'Something is surrounding us.'

'What? Where?'

'Everywhere.'

'What is it?'

'It is death. Can I ask you both a question?' Nano's shining eyes widened with dread. 'Everything has its opposite.'

'That is not a question, Nano,' Adam said.

'What,' Nano asked, 'is the opposite of AntGod?'

Some hours later, Nano spoke again. 'Master Adam?'

'Yes, Nano.'

'We have been living a lie.'

Adam murmured his agreement.

'Master Adam, can I ask you something?'

'Yes, Nano.'

'The alien ant left us with a threat.'

'Yes, he did.'

'Are we going to die?'

'Please stop, Nano.'

'I think we are, but not now.'

Zekiel sat up. 'When, Nano?'

'When they attack us.'

Much later that night, Nano spoke again. 'We are not all going to die.'

'I asked you to stop, Nano.'

'Most of us will, however.'

Adam felt the silent, throbbing darkness long after Nano and Zekiel had finally fallen asleep, a darkness so appalling he had to disentangle his feet and antennae from those of Nano and Zekiel lest his trembling body, horrified by what it sensed, woke them. Do you hear my cries, AntGod? In his mind's eye Adam saw the thousands of paths, tunnels and thoroughfares of AntLand, the innumerable store rooms, their thriving farms. He considered those meticulous processes through which the empire was administered, the systems of governance that had been refined over nearly 400 hundred months of laborious, meticulous endeavour, and how all that had been achieved could be destroyed in a day. All, he now saw, was frail. He lifted his face and prayed – he knew not to whom – imagining, as the words were whispered into the indifferent night, the raw terror of a godless world. Oblivion the empire once was; oblivion it could revert to. The world of aching abundance turned barren and breathless, the oppressive memories of the mad and the visionary dismissed by the nomadic, barbaric descendants of those few who might survive to wander nameless in a ravaged, desolate void.

He opened his eyes after completing his prayer to find Zekiel and Nano wide awake and looking at him. Nano asked Adam and Zekiel to sit close to him and form a tight circle. He rubbed together his abdominal joints, producing a song of mourning, one a little different to that created by the alien ants that grieved for their lost loved ones. And when his song had been sung, Nano, Adam and Zekiel sat looking one upon the other in silence for a long, long time.

Adam was the first to move. He stood and, making what was clearly an announcement, stated that he well understood that they had washed themselves earlier that day, and yet, despite this, they were to wash themselves again. He gave his instructions, which they carried out in an orderly, ceremonial manner, discharging saliva and daubing it over each other's head, jaws, thorax, abdomen and legs. After they were finished – despite not being hungry – Adam tapped repeatedly, first Zekiel's head, then Nano's; both in turn placed their mouth to Adam's mouth and regurgitated some of the food they had consumed earlier that night. Adam instructed Zekiel and Nano to do as he had done and, once those formalities were completed, the three of them stroked, nuzzled and caressed each other.

Chapter 9

Adam is Detained

Over two months later, Adam, Zekiel and Nano found themselves at the base of a steep embankment. They had retraced almost all of the 80,000 antbody lengths they had taken since the day they began their journey, using as their guide previously-laid scents, prominent features of the landscape and the sun. They were exhausted and emaciated, their taut bodies spent having eaten infrequently from their dwindling supply of food.

They struggled up the steep slope, stumbling with weariness. On several occasions, Zekiel fell, twisting both antennae and bruising his legs. And when at last they reached the highest point of that bank of earth they saw, far in the distance, the metropolis. The Royal Tower stood as an apparition encircled by a brightly-coloured ominous vapour that obscured its height. Work on the tower had continued apace, regardless, Adam knew, of thought or need or cost or, indeed, common sense. They ached for rest, but they were eager to return home, Adam and Young Nano inspired by Zekiel's determination to continue, despite the fact that his body shook, at times, as with a spasm. And so they tramped on without stopping, staggering with weariness, dragging themselves down a long embankment, leaning into the relentless heat and a shapeless, suppurating plume of stale vapour until, three days later and a few hours after midnight, they reached the entry of the tunnel from which they had made their escape over five months earlier.

Adam turned to Nano. 'You must return to your fellow workers.'

'I cannot. I must stay with you, Master.'

'Nano, you will, you must. I am releasing you from the pledge you made to yourself to protect me. No-one must know that you accompanied Zekiel and myself. The time will come when I'll need you. For now, save yourself.'

'You are going to inform The Council?'

'Yes, Nano.'

'They are not going to believe you.'

'They have to.'

'But they will not believe you.'

'Yes ... yes, you're right. But what else am I to do?'

'They will say you have lost your senses, Master.'

'After what we saw, I feel they might be correct.'

Nano stood. He hesitated. 'I had a dream last night, Master. I want to tell you about my dream, but I also do not want to tell you.'

'Tell me, then go, but be quick.'

'I am afraid to.'

'I want you to tell me.'

'No.'

'Are you truly afraid, Nano?'

'Yes and no, Master.'

'Explain yourself.'

'There are times when I am afraid because I know what is going to happen. Then there are times when I am not afraid because there is no uncertainty as to what is going to happen. I cannot unknow what I know. And I am sick, Master, because of what I hear. Do you hear?'

'No.'

'Zekiel? Do you hear?'

Zekiel watched Nano with his sad old eyes.

'What do you hear, Nano?' asked Adam.

'Are we civilised, Master?'

'What do you mean, Nano?'

'Are we civilised ants?'

'Why do you ask such a thing?'

'Zekiel?' Nano asked. 'Are we civilised?'

The aged sage rested one of his antennae on Nano's head.

'If we do not share our food with them, Master, and they attack us, will we kill them? If we do not share our supplies with ants who are starving to death, forcing them to attack us, does that we mean we can no longer claim to be civilised? I hear footsteps, Master, marching footsteps, the approach of death.'

'Oh, Nano, I am at a loss as to what to say to you,' said Adam. 'There will be time to discuss such matters later. I'll call for you when I need you. Now, do not argue. Do not disobey me. Leave us immediately.'

'Farewell, Master. Farewell, Zekiel the Wise.'

'Wait,' said Zekiel. 'Come to me.' Zekiel tapped Nano on the head, the young ant showing his acceptance of the old ant's loving-kindness by lowering both his antennae. Zekiel responded by placing his mouth over that of Nano's, after which he regurgitated half-digested lizard and snail flesh for the famished youngster. Zekiel then removed a piece of dried caterpillar meat from the fold in his thorax joint and presented it to Nano. You are, Zekiel thought, the word of AntGod, and if you, of all the ants in our empire, are not, then no ant charter with AntGod speaks the truth. 'Your fears are well-founded. The time for you to act is near. Eat well. AntLand and our Queen need you to stay strong. Farewell.'

Nano entered the tunnel. Zekiel gestured to a small puddle of water. 'Here, Master, drink.'

'No. I must go to the abandoned chambers. I want to drink from the water in those lower rooms.'

'Master, you need to rest. There will be difficult days ahead. Allow me to go.'

'We have little time, Zekiel. Collect the drips. You know why. Go now.'

On his return Zekiel folded back then lowered his antennae. He and Adam rubbed and kneaded each other's mouth, Adam drinking directly from that of his faithful servant. The water tasted sweet, pure and very cold. Its source was, Adam knew, that which flowed into the chasm he had almost fallen into.

'Here is the proof I had dreaded to find, Zekiel. Water melting from the snow-capped peaks of the cliffs is undermining the very foundations of our metropolis.'

Zekiel regurgitated the last of the honeydew he had kept in storage in his stomach, spitting it out at Adam's feet, offering it as a sign of his fealty and admiration. Adam ate the honeydew greedily. He sat there without speaking for a long time.

'Come,' said Zekiel, 'I shall accompany you to your chamber. You must rest. We must both rest.'

'No, Zekiel. I must see the Queen tonight. I fear that once AyJay Heartland knows of my return, I might be prevented from doing so. But before I go to her, I want you to make an inspection of the empire's food supplies so that I can give Her Majesty a full report. I dread what you'll find. I must stay in hiding until I see her, otherwise I would not ask you to do this. Go, my weary and exhausted friend. Return to me as soon as you have done so. I'll await you here.'

Zekiel returned two hours later. 'Our fungi, Master, they are ... I have never seen such a thing.'

'Tell me, Zekiel!'

'They are of a monstrous size.'

'From the heat?'

'I do not know. Perhaps. Should we assume so?'

'What of the odour?'

'Our farm workers are asleep, Master.'

'I know, Zekiel. Of course they are asleep! It's not what I asked you. What can you tell me of the odour, in the tunnels, the larders, the passages.'

'Many of our workers are wearing masks. I mean, Master, they are wearing masks while asleep.'

'Then the odour has become more intense.'

'Yes. It is more pungent. Lick my mandible, Master.'

The taste was caustic.

'And what of our aphids? Our greenflies? Our ladybirds?'

'Our supplies have dwindled.'

'And the old melia trees?'

'Skeletal.'

'All of them?'

'Not all. Many.'

'Then what are we feeding our livestock?'

'Reduced rations. And one thing more, Master.'

'What, Zekiel. Tell me.'

'May I suggest, while there is still time, that you come with me? There are some things I noticed that you must see so that you are able to convince the Queen that our fears are justified. Therein lies our future, Master.'

'You said I should make such an inspection while there's still time. What do you mean?'

'AyJay Heartland has discovered the tunnel in our absence. His pheromones are everywhere, on the walls, on the ground, informing every AntLander that the Queen rescinded her order that you survey the plains for a colony but you disobeyed her; that you used a secret passage intended only for Her Majesty to desert your post. He demands he be informed the moment you arrive in the metropolis.'

'Let's go, then, Zekiel.'

Prior to entering the tunnel, Zekiel took Adam to several vents. 'Are you making a reading, Master? Do you detect the output? Some of these vents are connected to those chambers in which leaves are fed to fungi, others to chambers where we store decomposing fungi.'

'Their release of the odour has become more acute in our absence, Zekiel.'

'Yes, Master. And there is something else. It is colder here,

Master, outside the metropolis.'

'I don't understand.'

'Come.'

They entered the tunnel.

'Do you feel how much warmer it is inside, Master? The warm odour rises, escaping through the vents, but it also seeps into the underground tunnel that opens up at the base of The Sacred Circle of Cliffs.'

'Then what? Is it our tunnels and thoroughfares providing pathways for the odour to escape into The Eternal Valley? Of course! And then there are the discharges from the waste dumps that The Queen had asked me to inspect. What does this mean? Between the odours we are producing inside and outside ...'

'There is something else, Master. I went to the quarters in which eggs and larvae were once transported to protect them from the cold. The quarters were empty. And the contingent of workers previously assigned to care for the eggs and larvae were nowhere to be seen.'

'I don't understand, Zekiel. This contingent had been disbanded *because* they weren't needed. It's no longer so cold in the empire that the eggs and larvae *need* to be transferred anywhere.'

'That unit of workers still exists.'

'There are things you don't know, Zekiel. The Council decided many months before you and I departed to disband this group. The eggs and larvae aren't being transferred anywhere but remain in their place of birth and development.'

'No, they are still being transported elsewhere. I know this to be true, Master.'

'Zekiel, we're wasting time. The worker-ants wouldn't take it upon themselves to take such an initiative, and The Council had decided otherwise.'

'Forgive me, Master. You are wrong. You have been misled. Believe me, I beg of you. They are being carried out of the chambers in which they matured.'

'You were told or you saw this with your own eyes?'

'I saw. With my own eyes, Master.'

'And taken where?'

'I do not know.'

'Why hadn't you told me?'

'The worker in charge told me it had been The Council Elders who had made this decision. I assumed you knew. I assumed you had taken part in the discussion with your fellow Elders.'

'This is disturbing, Zekiel. I must speak to the workers who do the transporting. Where are their living quarters?'

'I do not know. The workers were forbidden from revealing the location of their living quarters.'

'What? But why? Why would such a thing be kept secret?'

'They had been made to take an oath.'

'No!'

'Yes, Master. There is great secrecy about both: I mean, the location of the eggs and larvae and the quarters of the workers who transport them and care for them.'

'Zekiel, we go to the Royal Chamber to see the Queen. Now. I must tell her what's happening with the empire's governance. Come.'

'Master, no-one is permitted to approach without A Royal

Invitation. Your way will be barred. The Imperial Runners will apprehend you.'

'We can no longer exercise caution, Zekiel. There's too much at stake. Follow me.'

The series of Royal Obeisance Stations leading to the inner sanctum of the Queen's residence, where subjects were required to kneel and proclaim their obedience to the Queen, were normally heavily guarded. The first of these, however, was unguarded. Adam and Zekiel exchanged looks of concern. Why would this be so?

They continued. The passageway echoed with their voices and Zekiel's tottering footsteps. They made their way hesitantly to the second, then the third station – all stood eerily silent. Two sleeping Imperial Runner doorkeepers lay at the entrance to The Royal Chamber itself. Their enormous heads were disc-shaped and, placed side by side, formed a tightly-fitting doorway to the chamber. Adam took tentative steps, sniffing the air. His olfactory message to Zekiel awoke one of the Runners who immediately leapt to his feet.

'Elder Adam, forgive me, but you are not permitted entry.'

'Where's the Queen?'

'Elder Adam! No-one is allowed ——'

Adam Ant brushed past the Runner, pushed open the door to The Royal Chamber and entered. The Queen, her carers, those charged with guarding her, those with transporting the eggs she produced each day to incubating chambers – all were gone.

'I am sorry, Elder Adam, but I have to report you,' the

Runner cried, as Adam ran past him. 'Under pain of death I have been told to report you to AyJay Heartland! Forgive me, please!'

Adam rushed to the depot where the leaves his foragers collected were taken for processing. Zekiel followed some distance behind. They went to the individual rooms in which small ants cut the dwindling supply of leaves into fragments, then to the vaults where these pieces were crushed and moulded into pellets. They went to the chambers where the fungi bed were tended. Adam tested the air in each room, scanned the ground and the walls. The largest vault was almost completely filled with decomposing fungi. He stood erect, his antennae twitching and pulling and contracting, feeling the atmosphere with every nerve, not only in his antennae but also in his legs and abdomen and mandibles. He realised that the breakdown of the soil was contributing to the release of the odour into the atmosphere. It was, he knew, the same odour he had first become aware of on the occasion of the Queen's address.

After awaking his managers, Adam asked for statistics comparing harvests over the previous 120 months. Once he received these, he gave the order that henceforth hourly readings of the composition of the air be conducted and forwarded to him. He stared hard at the decomposing organic materials and saw, with his own eyes, detected, with his own body, the release of perversely odorous vapours: in small quantities, yes, but if one vapour was to merge with another, if they were to escape the rooms, travel through tunnels and form one mighty body ...

'Master,' said one of his managers, 'we are under instructions to report your return to Elder AyJay.'

'Do what you must do. Zekiel, we have little time. Come.'

They took the path down to the city's deepest chambers which, Adam knew, had been proclaimed by the ChairAnt many months previously to be out of bounds. Adam stood with Zekiel at the ledge from which he was once able to look down onto a vast network of passages and tunnels, connecting rooms, chambers and vaults – a city within a city. The entire area was now completely submerged in water. A peculiarly-coloured phosphorescent cloud drifted like some premonition of death over the vast underground sea. This dark, lifeless, still body of water had overwhelmed what had been a vital part of the empire. Adam tasted the water. It was icy cold. He scanned the odour. It was similar to the odour he had detected in The Royal Forest. The water had melted from the snow-capped tower, flowed down into a chasm and, through some network of tunnels, found its way into these chambers.

He instructed Zekiel to go immediately to each of the Elders and, with Adam's pheromonal authority, inform them that there was to be a Council meeting the following day and that it was imperative the Queen be present.

He went alone to The Imperial Gate. The Royal Tower stood, thankfully incomplete, some 300 antbodies high, a testament to ant genius and folly and the manifestation of AyJay Heartland's arrogance.

Above the entrance to the metropolis, inscribed in enormous letters, were words that must have been unveiled at some ceremonial occasion during his absence. He read them over and over.

Come, let us build ourselves a tower, with its peak in the heavens, and let us make a name for ourselves that will be our glory in the glorious history of AntLand.

Another huge sign, which referred to the structure as a *heavenscraper*, loudly reminded all of the Queen's motto: *Bigger! Better! Best!* A third gave details of the projected height of *that marvellous, glorious, AyJay Heartland-inspired edifice*, the complexity of its air-cooling system – designed by the ChairAnt himself – and the various sites in The Eternal Valley that would be mined for materials to be used for the tower's façade.

Adam left to examine the empire's huge disposal sites, each one of which was approximately 120 antbodies high. He sat, observing in silence, thinking, thinking. He took readings, then scanned the air.

The gathering of all manner of plants by his own foragers, he realised, had caused great damage. He himself, he thought with great shame, had wreaked havoc on the plant life of the valley, never once discriminating between what was fresh and what was old, what was needed and what could be ignored: if it was green, he had ordered his foragers to harvest it.

Even worse was AyJay HeartLand's most recent act of vandalism. After examining some of the vast quantities of pheromonic emissions from those workers who had laboured on the site, Adam came to understand what AyJay Heartland had done: so that the tower would achieve the prominence he desired, he had instructed thousands of Adam's hunters to bite into the base of the veins supplying nourishment to every leaf of every plant within a vast radius of the metropolis; once they had bitten into the veins, other hunters had injected a stream of poison from the end of their abdomens into the open wound. An enormous area around the empire was becoming a wasteland so that The Royal Tower would stand unobstructed from view.

Adam walked here and there and made calculations from a variety of positions, constantly altering his perspective. Each reading produced the same result: the vast refuse dumps teemed with toxins. He thought back to the sensation in his nerves when he had detected the release of gas in the fungi rooms and the gaseous cloud that had killed his fellow AntLanders. They had the same composition, only differing in intensity. The revelations struck him like a physical blow. The heating of the empire was a fact and it was increasing, not only in the metropolis, but also in the entire Eternal Valley. The clouds of vapour did not die but were being contained in the valley by The Sacred Circle of Cliffs. The gases that they themselves produced had destroyed the forests, melted the snow, poisoned the air.

He returned and, at The Imperial Gate, gazed once more in horror and wonder at The Royal Tower. Construction, he knew, had to cease. What had been built had to be destroyed. Ideas of growth had to be discarded. Those millions of workers conscripted into its building had to be re-employed into schemes that would save the empire. It was imperative that the Queen be persuaded to produce far fewer offspring. The ingenuity of the ant had to refocus. He made for the entry into the construction site of the tower, but his way was barred by an Imperial Runner, who told him it was dangerous to enter.

Adam retired to his chamber exhausted. There were, he knew, too many ants, too much loading of gases into the atmosphere ... AntLand was, simply, overcrowded.

He heard a noise. Several Imperial Runners burst into his room.

'You do not enter the private room of an Elder uninvited!' Adam said. 'Leave. Leave immediately.'

'We seek your pardon, Elder Adam. The manner of our entry was one determined by another. You have been summoned. There is to be a meeting of The Council of Elders.'

'I am well aware of that. I'm the one who called for it. You're in error. It's to occur tomorrow. Now, leave me be.'

'Again, Elder Adam, we beg your pardon. We have been instructed to inform you that your request has been denied. You are to accompany us to The Council Chamber. You must go immediately. An Extraordinary Meeting of Elders is being held tonight.'

Chapter 10

Adam is Reprimanded

What to tell them? That there existed alien life beyond the cliffs? That the empire needed to depopulate in order to survive? And what of the yellow ant's greeting, request and threat?

When he arrived at the threshold of The Council Chamber, he knew immediately that he faced a hostile meeting: Assistant-Elder Gredo had taken Adam's normal position; no-one looked at Adam as he entered and no-one responded to his greeting. Adam was puzzled to see that the ChairAnt stood outside the circle of Elders, watching in silence from a corner.

Gredo scanned Adam's pheromones. 'You lost 100 of our AntLanders?'

'Where am I to stand?'

'I asked you a question. Your pheromones betray you. Answer me. Is it true that you lost 100 of our finest?'

'Yes, and you have taken my position in this Council. Please move.'

'A hundred of our fellow AntLanders, I say, 100 whom

you had no authority to take with you! Dead, Elder Adam, dead because of you. And you're more concerned about your position at this meeting being taken, when clearly an explanation is required regarding the tragic fate of our fellow ants.' The Assistant-Elder looked about the room, his pleasure exuding through his antennae.

'We stopped by The Queen's Lake and ——'

'We? Are you implicating Zekiel the Wise in their deaths? When it was you who absconded from our metropolis and conscripted both Zekiel and those 100 innocents?' Gredo addressed the Elders. 'Here we have the youngest ever Elder in the long history of AntLand, whom our Queen has misjudged by anointing him as the one to assume ChairAnt AyJay Heartland's position when our revered Elder retires. Here we have the Elder who took it upon himself to disobey our Queen and depart from our metropolis, despite the fact Her Highness rescinded her command that he explore the plains and choose a site for a new colony. You, Adam Ant, have failed in your duty as an obedient servant of our Queen!'

'The valley is in crisis,' said Adam. 'I've seen the warning signs. Something is seriously wrong. The forests are retreating. Poisonous gases stalk the deforested valley floor. We are producing prodigious amounts of potent vapours in our farmlands and our compost heaps that escape through our own vents. The weather has become unpredictable. The temperature is rising and so the snow and ice on The Sacred Circle of Cliffs is melting. The consequence? Water is flowing directly beneath our city.'

'Elder Adam! We are only seven months from our 400th anniversary celebrations. We cannot, we will not, be distracted from our plans, nor are we interested in your wild and unfounded ——'

Adam's six limbs and both of his antennae ached at their joints. He had open wounds that needed healing. He had never known such weariness and desperately needed several days' rest and sleep. Were these the reasons, he would ask himself later, that he cut Assistant-Elder Gredo off and blurted out what he'd told himself he would keep to himself until he'd had an audience with the Queen? 'If this deterioration continues we won't be able to feed ourselves! Parts of the valley have turned to desert. Everywhere Zekiel the Wise and I went we saw signs of ...' He paused. He turned to look at the ChairAnt, who had remained standing in a darkened corner.

AyJay Heartland spoke. 'Signs of what, Elder Adam?'

Adam could sense the ChairAnt's sly disdain. The smugness exuded from his limbs, the smirking arrogance distorting his antennae.

'Crisis, you say? AntLand unable to feed its citizens? Oh, dear, please enlighten us, then. What exactly are you saying these are signs of?'

Too late, too late, Adam thought. Oh, fool that I am! Why had I not remained silent?

'We await your thoughts. How we long for the wisdom of one as young and inexperienced as our Elder Adam.' He waited. 'Silence, Elder Adam? Nothing to say? After sneaking out of our metropolis, being absent from your sacred duties for an unconscionable period of time, an absence which led to the unhealthily enormous size of our fungi and the undernourished distorted limbs of our melia trees, you are unable to give this body of Elders an explanation for your actions? You, the ant responsible for the deaths of 100 of our fellow AntLanders, dare to communicate nothing but pheromones of contempt for your august peers? Take note.' He paused to look hard into the eyes of each of the Elders in turn with his menacing, heavy-lidded, shifting eyes. 'And remember, always, that this recalcitrant is, at this very moment, looking upon us as if we are ignorant and dull-witted, and why? Because we do not share his wild views. We await, Elder Adam.' His antennae bristled. 'Are you afraid to speak?'

'I fear the valley cannot continue to sustain us. I fear that the vast amount of flora we carry into our metropolis and the huge piles of our excrement, our dead and our rejected food scraps are changing the nature of the soil of The Eternal Valley. I fear that our empire faces its demise.'

Elder AyJay smiled, an infrequent thing for the ChairAnt. It was, Adam thought, a smile that was no smile at all.

'I see. The valley has lost some of its trees, the temperature has risen and you think that a civilisation such as ours is threatened.' He looked at each Elder with eyes he made cold and calculating, pausing to emphasise that great authority he had over them. 'We have never had a problem feeding our own. We have twelve months' reserves of food and you are saying ... What was it, Elder Adam? That AntLand faces its *demise*?' He chuckled without mirth, his dark face stone hard. 'These are unsubstantiated, baseless, ill-founded claims that are distracting us from the purpose of this meeting, claims that are unbefitting of one whom the Queen sees as my successor. You are not well, Elder Adam. You need rest. And now to the purpose of this meeting: you are hereby informed that this Council is charged with the grave responsibility of conducting an official enquiry into your behaviour to ascertain whether you are a fit and proper ant to maintain the position of an Elder. Our Royal Commission begins tomorrow. You are dismissed. You are to go directly to your chamber. You are to remain there until you are summoned.'

'But I must see the Queen.'

'No, you must not see the Queen. You will not see the Queen. *You* do not tell *me* what you must do and whom you will see. You are to retire to your quarters and remain there until further notice.'

'The idea of limitless growth is ——'

'Zekiel the Wise! Enter!'

Zekiel opened the door to The Council Chamber. 'Your actions, Elder Adam, could have cost our Sage his life. Escort this ant to his quarters, Zekiel. The meeting is adjourned.'

'AyJay Heartland is preventing me from seeing the Queen, Zekiel.'

'Her Majesty is not the only one whom you cannot see, Master. I have been instructed to ensure you remain in your chamber.'

'But why you, Zekiel? Do you think it's a trap? That they've given you, of all ants, the responsibility of guarding me?'

'No, Master. They discharged pheromones indicating their ignorance of our relationship. We are, for the time being, safe.'

'Then we could try and find her. I mean, we could go now.'

'Yes, we could. But, Master Adam, where would we begin

to look? We would be found, I would be removed from my position and an Imperial Runner would be charged with guarding you. And I? I would almost certainly be executed.'

'Zekiel, why would someone spirit the Queen from The Royal Chamber? What benefit would there be? We assume AyJay Heartland is responsible for this, don't we?'

'I am at a loss to think what he is planning, Master.'

'Secretly transferring the eggs and larvae to an undisclosed site has something to do with whatever he's planning. I fear it, Zekiel, I fear it.'

'As do I. But there are, for the time being, other issues causing me grief.' He paused. 'I have been ordered to make a report of our journey.'

'I don't want you to suffer unduly. Tell them most of what we know. Omit nothing but the presence of the alien ants and our setting foot onto The Sacred Circle. We have to think about how we're to reveal all of what we know. We can't afford to become a laughing-stock of the entire empire. And yet, we don't have much time! Oh, Zekiel, how do we convince our AntLanders of the reality of what we saw? And yet, why *would* they believe us? You and I had never considered the possibility that there might be other ants, so why should they? And what then? When we do tell all to all – as we inevitably must – and are met with incredulity, derision and laughter, what will be the consequences for the empire? And to me? And of course to you? I regret the troubles I've created for you, Zekiel. Forgive me.'

'There is nothing to forgive, Master. The reason they have misjudged our relationship is because they believe I was conscripted along with those ants who perished. The Elders believe that I had no choice but to accompany you.'

'Well, Zekiel, this is true. After all, you *were* following my and the Queen's instructions.'

'They will be pleased to hear you did not discover a site for a new colony.'

'How disappointed the Queen will be to learn of my failure.'

'Perhaps. Perhaps not. She believes in you, Master.'

'A faith I do not merit. And so, old ant, what do your wise old bones tell you? Where will all this end?'

Zekiel bowed his head and nodded gravely several times. 'Master.'

'Yes, Zekiel.'

'I also have great faith in you.'

'Thank you, Zekiel, but you've not answered my question.'

'I shall tell you this: the Queen is not alone. I have heard she keeps company with a newly hatched princess, who is a delight to our Queen.'

'I'm glad to hear that, Zekiel. But what has that to do with what I asked you?'

'The young give hope to the old. It is the nature of existence. It is what AntGod intended. The Queen instructed me to accompany you. You and Her Majesty both honour me. I am grateful to have been chosen.'

Chosen in more ways than one, Adam thought. Now it is I who think in riddles.

Chapter 11

AyJay Heartland, The Grand Inquisitor

Late afternoon the following day, Adam was summoned to The Council Chamber and ordered to give a report on what he had seen in The Royal Forest. He described the enormous bubbles of gas and the deaths of his fellow JourneyAnts. He told of the water flowing into the chasm and of the link between that river and the flooding in the deepest chambers in the metropolis. He omitted all references to his sighting of the aliens. There was a long silence in the room once he had finished his report.

AyJay Heartland finally spoke. 'You say you went into the deep chambers?'

'Yes.'

'You went into areas which are out of bounds.'

'Yes, but Elder AyJay, I am ——'

'And you abandoned procedure when you left your fellow ants and our Zekiel in a hostile environment so that you could ... do what? Elder Adam, you have not yet satisfactorily explained to The Council why you abandoned your AntLanders. Where did you go? Did you, perhaps, approach The Sacred Circle of Cliffs?'

'What are you implying?'

AyJay Heartland sniggered again without mirth and then spoke with the haughty manner and contemptuous tone that made the Elders afraid of him. 'Take note, my fellow Councillors, how this ant has avoided answering my question by asking a question. Your deceit does not escape me, Adam Ant. You disobey the Queen and now you disobey me. Deceit upon deceit. Oh, how well I know your kind. I know you to be a recalcitrant. AntGod alone knows how Zekiel the Wise was able to suffer your egotism. You have yet to explain why you did not obey the Queen when she rescinded her command.'

'I was not told! I did not know! In fact, I do not believe the Queen ——'

'It is your duty to know. Ignorance of the law does not absolve you. If we allow you to go unpunished, what authority will we have over the Queen's subjects? To accept your paltry defence leads us to chaos. Is this not so?' He paused before resting his many unblinking eyes on Assistant-Elder Gredo, swinging his antennae from side to side. 'Is this, I say, not so?'

'I believe,' began the Assistant-Elder, 'that ——'

AyJay Heartland turned to look at him with his dark, sullen face. 'A motion from you indicating accordance with my views suffices.'

The ChairAnt waited until he had received a nod of agreement then proceeded, twisting threateningly his antennae, to stare at each Council member in turn until he had received a gesture of consensus from each. 'This is extraordinary, Adam Ant. No-one has ever defied the Queen, as you have done, and here you stand, refusing to give a full account of all your actions, of how, for example, you had placed Zekiel the Wise in the unenviable position of having to obey you rather than our Queen. And are you, by the way, aware of the poor physical state Zekiel is in because of you? Shame on you, Adam Ant! Your conduct has been disgraceful. We seek an explanation – now.'

All eyes and antennae were now upon Adam. He felt the hostility in the room. 'No-one has the authority to deny an Elder access to the Queen. I demand, as is my right, to see Her Majesty.'

'And you continue to ignore me. And so, my Council of Elders, take further note: this renegade ignores your ChairAnt's demands that he give an explanation of his actions. Here is my response, Elder Adam. You are clearly hiding something. Further to that, take special note: one who does not have the support of a single Elder – or Zekiel, I might add; yes, Adam Ant, I have spoken to him and he has no kind words to say about you – no-one, I say, who stands alone, particularly a deceitful renegade such as yourself, is in a position to make demands. It is the opinion of this Council that you are not fit to be an Elder, let alone my successor. We shall be recommending your immediate removal from The Council of Elders to Her Majesty once you have faced the full force of our law.'

'I now know why we're having such long periods of extreme heat,' said Adam.

'That is not the issue. That is not why this meeting has been convened. This Council is not interested in your green fascist views. What next, Elder Adam? That we have to devise new ways of breathing?' AyJay laughed and, looking again into the eyes of the other Elders, invited them to join with him in ridiculing Adam. They shifted uneasily, looking one to the other hesitantly, before breaking into laughter.

'I know the consequences of allowing these gases to proliferate.'

'You see,' said AyJay, addressing The Council, 'ants like Adam here would have us reduce our population, our livestock, even our food supplies. It is true, is it not, Elder Adam? The consequence of acting on your advice would be a smaller empire, would it not?'

Silence.

AyJay Heartland's mood shifted, becoming dark, stern and cold. 'Let us be clear as to what is involved here. Given the opportunity, you would be arguing for a smaller AntLand, yes? Nothing to say? We do not want to hear your doomsday reports. Your silence betrays your intentions, Elder Adam. This meeting has come to an end.' He called for Zekiel. 'Once The Council has departed, escort this obdurate ant to his room.'

Led by the ChairAnt, the Elders filed out in strict order.

Once out of the chamber and in the passageway, Adam absorbed the pheromones of the Elders. He sensed their mockery of all that he had said. 'Our fears are well-founded, Zekiel. No-one is taking me seriously. Unless we find the whereabouts of the Queen, we're doomed. Our subject ants will listen to her but not to me. Where can she be?'

'It is a great mystery, Master. Rumours are rife, but they lead nowhere. I cannot risk my relationship with the ChairAnt by asking him such a question. He thinks you repulse me, Master. He must continue to think that he has my support. There is much you need to forgive me for.'

'You? Again you ask for forgiveness? Never, Zekiel.'

'Ah, but you are not present to hear what I have to say about you, Master.'

'And so you must continue. If not to gain his confidence, at the very least to protect yourself. What's behind AyJay Heartland's scheming, Zekiel?'

'We have more than that to fear, Master.'

'The greeting,' said Adam.

'The request,' added Zekiel.

And as one, they said: 'The yellow ant's threat.'

Adam was returned to his room. He lay down, exhausted, and quickly fell into a deep sleep.

A few hours later, when all was quiet, still and dark, he was awoken by someone prodding him. It was Zekiel.

'What is it?' said Adam. 'What's wrong?'

'You must get up. Now.' Zekiel left the room.

Sitting in a corner and watching Adam was AyJay Heartland. Adam sat up, shook his mandibles and antennae then rubbed them to see if he was imagining things. But it was not some trick of the mind, the eye or the antenna. AyJay Heartland sat, staring, observing him with his brilliant, black eyes.

'Why are you here?' asked Adam.

The ChairAnt relaxed his antennae. He released pheromones of disdain.

'What do you want?'

AyJay Heartland stirred, crossed an antennae over the

other then returned it to its previous position. 'Do you absorb my scorn, Adam Ant? Yes? No? Are you wondering why I would view you with odium? Perhaps that is too strong a word. Let us settle on ... Let me see ... What about contempt? Yes, I believe that is an appropriate word. You see, there are ways one might behave that could lead to one achieving one's aims, but to challenge a system so entrenched as ours, to do battle against those who have managed, over a great period of time, to place themselves at the summit of such a system, in the process having those beneath them reliant on their superior for their position, their status, the many benefits they enjoy ... well, Adam Ant, such a fool deserves to be looked upon with contempt if he has not learnt to play by certain rules.'

'Is that what you have come to my chamber to tell me?'

'Oh, not at all. Speaking in this way to someone like you, an ant vanquished, shall we say, is one of the benefits of influence. You saw for yourself the power I have over the Elders. Treat them with contempt, speak to them with a tongue that is arrogant, rebuke them as if they are children and they become as obedient as ... well, as children. Of course, one may behave this way only if one has chosen as one's underlings those who are easily intimidated. You see, to sustain his total authority, a leader must rule with some brutality. Those who are ruled must fear the one who rules. He certainly has to be capricious, at times even impenetrable. And from his lofty position, Adam Ant, that ruler will not only be obeyed but, dare I say, also venerated. You do understand that one may only speak in the manner in which I am speaking to you if one does so from a position of strength. Rules, Adam Ant, rules. You never did learn the intricate complexities of powerplay.

'I have come to inform you of ... How shall I put it? ... certain changes that have occurred in your absence. I also have a number of unsolved problems, questions, shall we say, that I want you to answer. No, do not speak. You will not speak. You are not required to speak yet. This is not a conversation. This is, for the time being ... How shall I phrase it? ... a situation, let us say, of my speaking and of you listening.

'Let us begin by considering what happened to you during that period when you were absent from our city. What is a concern to the Elders, but not to me, I hasten to add, is that you lost 100 AntLanders. What interests me is that you managed to save your own life and that of Zekiel's. I am curious as to what happened to claim the lives of so many but not your own. A strange thing, I say. I repeat, a strange thing. Now you may speak, Adam Ant.'

'I shall speak to the Queen, not to you.'

'Of course you will not speak to me, because I am now certain that you *do* have something to hide. I am correct, am I not?'

Silence.

'Ah, but your silence speaks.'

'Does Her Majesty know of my return?'

'Oh, our Queen is busying herself with her princess. She says she is imparting all that she knows to her little one. Does she know you have returned? Adam Ant, do not flatter yourself that our Queen concerns herself with thoughts of you.

'Now, let us consider a few matters. You return a failure and you refuse to explain why you did not do as you had been instructed. No, no, no, do not speak: you do not need to tell me that you were not aware of the Queen rescinding her directions. I know she had not. Of course, not all the Elders are aware of this. Some suspect that to be the case, but they are too frightened to speak their minds. That issue has no relevancy here. What is relevant, however, is that you also went into the deep chambers of the city when you know such areas are out of bounds. You approached what had formerly been The Royal Obeisance Stations without a Royal Invitation and then ... and then you entered what had been The Royal Chamber itself. You even attempted to enter The Royal Tower's building site. What a curious ant you are. Did you not think that I would find out, that I would be told? You behave as if you have already assumed the position of ChairAnt.

'You need to know, Adam Ant, that I am here with the Queen's approval. Ahhh, you smile. Let me rephrase what I just said. I am here having told the Elders that I am acting on Her Majesty's behalf. I trust you understand the significance of what I just told you.' He hardened his antennae and distended his abdomen to make it appear as large as possible. 'Now, listen to me, you upstart. As of two months ago, contact with the Queen can only be made through me. Council meetings can only be called by me, or with my approval. Do you see, Adam Ant, what has been achieved in your absence?

You, Adam Ant, are an affront to the dignity of an Elder, one Elder in particular – me. I think you know that what you said at our Council meeting has made you a figure of ridicule.

'Let me, then, be as clear as I can possibly be.' He stood, leaned over Adam, then swept his antennae from side to side, emitting intense, threatening chemical discharges. 'There is much about ant nature that you do not understand. Indeed, Adam Ant, you are a threat to our wellbeing. There are a number of reasons why you are being detained. That is one of them. Building The Royal Tower gives each subject something to dream of, something to hope for. It is the physical manifestation of all that is the antithesis of despair. When it is completed, they will be overwhelmed with pride. The operative words, Adam Ant, are that *they will be overwhelmed*. They, in their wholesome stupidity, are made happy by the act of a dream, an aspiration, being realised in front of their very eyes: the biggest ant-made structure in the entire universe.

'I believe this or, should I say, I choose to believe this. Its construction is, for them, a necessary mindless distraction. They have neither the time nor energy to be curious or to think critically. You, on the other hand, would attempt to raise their consciousness. I can feel it in your pheromones now, this very moment: *life*, you are thinking, *was not meant to be this way*.

'You would say that we in AntLand have satisfied our physical need for shelter and food, and that we should now devote our energies to the satisfying of higher, more idealistic goals. You would have your fellow AntLanders delight in their very existence. You would encourage them to query our origins, ask questions regarding the birthplace and parentage of the Queen and what that means for our place in the universe, even become curious about the very existence of AntGod. Oh, yes, I know how your mind works, Adam Ant. You would try to reverse the natural inclination to stupidity, attempt to have all the ants questioning, creating existential needs that can *never* be satisfied. Ne-ver, I say. You would create a vacuum whereas I, on the other foot, am creating a tower. How is it that you have not learnt that dissatisfaction leads to despair? Why is it that you would encourage your fellow AntLanders to question, rather than motivating them to accept the notion that things happen for a reason? I am correct in making that assumption, am I not?

'In the weeks after our Queen made The Eternal Valley her own, her ovaries heavy, she laid her eggs in the chamber which she herself had dug. Her first brood of workers raised her offspring. Out of her twenty ovaries she gave birth to those workers who knew without thinking that they were the lifeblood of AntLand. They worked together as a wonderfully well-organised community. They did not need to be told their function. They did not question. They gave themselves obediently. They behaved altruistically. No-one questioned, Adam Ant, what destiny had determined for them, not the workers nor, dare I say, our Queen herself, who created her chamber at the predestined depth of 400 antbody lengths. Did she have to be told to dig to that depth? No. Aphids do not turn into butterflies. Bees do not metamorphose into spiders. Young Elders do not defy those who are their seniors. There are central principles that regulate ant behaviour which you do not appreciate, do not value – indeed, which you openly flout. Do you see why you have been made a prisoner in your own chamber?

'If the order with which AntLand is governed were to be disrupted – because *that*, Adam Ant, is one of the issues at stake – The Eternal Valley would become ill-disposed towards us. Loathsome epidemics would sweep through our disposal sites and cemeteries, our farms would be neglected, leading to starvation, the authority of those maintaining order would be challenged. There is a reason, you see – or, should I say, there is a reason you clearly do not see – why random events are not permitted to disrupt the order of our world.

'I suspect you have cultivated a peculiar respect for trees and the like. The veneration I sense you have acquired for nature is an obstacle to AntLand's dominion over the inferior creatures AntGod has provided for us. I do not doubt that the temperature is rising, Elder Adam. I do not doubt the presence of this odour. I have eyes. I have antennae. I have nerves. I see what you see. I feel what you feel. The most opportune recourse for us in meeting these problems is through growth. We have to be fruitful. We must multiply. It is a gift, given to us – indeed, it is our destiny – to conquer and have dominion over the entire Eternal Valley.' He leant forward. 'We are as powerful and as creative as gods, Adam Ant.'

Yes, we are, Adam thought sadly, and we have to get better at it.

'Our empire can be as large as we desire it to be. No problem of ant destiny is beyond AntLand. Our methods, our planning, our finesse, the logic and reasoning abilities of those of us who have been chosen to lead, all have enabled us to conquer this valley. Do you really believe we cannot use ant ingenuity to overcome any challenge? The ingenuity, I mean, of ants such as myself. After all we have done, do you have so little faith in your own kind? We have manipulated much of the valley largely to our will. We have exploited our surrounds to suit our needs. We have moulded natural forces to create this vast empire. No problem of ant destiny is beyond AntLand.' He placed his face up against Adam's. 'Do our subjects not believe that we are the masters of the universe?' he said, with a conviction and hostility that frightened Adam. 'Do they not live a life without fears?

'As for our subject-ants, you now understand that I do not want them to think. How is it that no-one has ever asked where the Queen came from? How is it that it has never occurred to any ant to wonder about the identity of the ant who, after the Queen departed the nest of her birth and took to the air, fastened his legs around her body to inseminate her and what that means for our claim to be the masters of the universe? I am saying that it has never occurred to any of our subjects to ask these questions and what they imply. But that is not true, is it, because there is one amongst us – apart from myself, of course – to have asked such questions, and that is you. Is that not the case, Adam Ant? As for our subject-ants, they do not realise it, but they themselves do not *want* to think. For most of them, the examined life, Adam Ant, is not worth living.

'Do you see, Adam Ant? Do you agree? You may speak.'
Silence.
'Not responding will not assist you. You see, that is

primarily why I am here: to hear you say "Yes, ChairAnt AyJay Heartland, I see. Yes, I agree." You, Adam Ant, have the opportunity to live the privileged life of an Elder. You can choose to resume your position as Royal Forager and Grand Protector of Food Supplies. To do so, however, you must proclaim what I want to hear and, once you have regained your freedom, behave in the appropriate manner.'

'Where's the Queen?'

'With her princess, as I previously told you. That is your response?'

'Where have you taken her?'

'Will you submit to me?'

'I demand to see our Queen.'

AyJay Heartland shuffled his feet and rubbed his mandibles together. His mood darkened. 'Fool! You are to remain in your chamber until I have determined the day when you will have to answer for your insubordination. You will, however, be given other opportunities to recant your heretical views and openly, clearly, unambiguously admit to the error of your ways and, of course, submit to The Council – and, of course, to me, Adam Ant. Acknowledge your misdemeanours, reject the notion of ever succeeding me, accept my full authority. What do you say?'

'Never.'

'I have wasted my time with you. And now, what am I to do with you? The Queen, misguidedly, looks upon you fondly. Many of your foragers and protectors of our food supplies, I have been told, resist looking upon you with anything but affection. But you never fooled me, Adam Ant. I saw you for the schemer you are when you dispatched that bee, which was already in its death throes. Adam Ant, the so-called hero, commended by our Queen. Bah!' The ChairAnt walked towards the exit, stopped, turned to face Adam and, making narrow his eyes, said with a sly sense of delight, 'Everyone would have thought you were insane if you had said everything you wanted to say. You do know that, do you not?'

'I don't know what you mean.'

'Oh, you know very well what I mean. And now you know that I know.'

'I spoke honestly. I said what was on my mind.'

'Yes, that is your problem, Adam Ant. But you withheld, did you not? It is a wonder you did not lose all self-control and tell The Council that ... Now, let me see, what might it have been? Oh, yes, that you came across aliens.'

In the weeks that followed, withering heat spells and a thick mist lingering malevolently around the building site caused many worker ants to collapse and some to expire. The glowing clouds swelled in depth and density. The death rate climbed, particularly amongst the youngest and the oldest. The water level in the bowels of the city rose. Work on The Royal Tower, however, did not cease.

Hearing of the accelerating deforestation of the valley and the spot fires breaking out near the metropolis' disposal sites, Adam sent Zekiel out to investigate on a daily basis. Zekiel saw the sunwhitened remains of trees standing upright and ghostly and felt a dry breeze whistling through branches that cracked and groaned. On one oppressive day, he dug a hole deep enough to burrow into so that he could escape the relentless heat and the solemn, still spectre of the appalling odour.

Soon after, Zekiel discovered that a pheromonic message had been left for him. The identity of the messenger was unmistakable. The yellow alien's pheromones informed him that the rumours of a land of plenty, spread by a bee that, several months previously, had the opportunity to see with its own eyes the abundant supply of food in AntLand, had spread far and wide. Adam was told that a response to his request was required. *Go back to your Queen*, the pheromones said. *Tell her what you know. We have little time.* The yellow ant's threat was also repeated.

Adam linked antennae with Zekiel. Their thoughts dissolved then merged so that what Zekiel knew, Adam learnt. United in this way, they determined that together, come what may, they had to leave Adam's chamber immediately and find the Queen. They exited Adam's chambers to inform Her Majesty of the yellow ant's dire warning, only to be confronted by the arrival of several Imperial Runners, sent to escort Adam to The Council Chamber.

Chapter 12

Adam Ant's Blasphemy

The Imperial Runners, marching in two lines, led Adam to an anteroom. At its entrance, he was instructed to wait in silence until he was summoned into the chamber. He stood for several hours, during which time he heard no sound from behind the closed door.

It was well into the night when he finally detected, in the far distance, the shuffling echo of many feet stepping in time. Several minutes later, the entire Council of Elders arrived. At their head was AyJay Heartland. The Council members trooped in strict order through the antechamber, legs striding, antennae swaying in time, eyes looking stiffly ahead. They paused at the entry to The Council Chamber, marching in military fashion on the spot, waiting until an Imperial Runner strutted to the door and threw it open. The Elders entered. The door was loudly slammed shut.

Many more hours passed until, finally, the door was opened abruptly and a gruff voice from within barked its summons to Adam. After he entered, one of the Elders closed the door then bolted it. The Council members were sitting at a rectangular-shaped table. Two of them broke from the group, seized Adam by his front legs and escorted him to the head of this table. AyJay Heartland moved from his position and stood directly behind Adam, so close that the younger Elder could feel AyJay's mandibles on his rear legs. The ChairAnt moved his antennae in a slow, deliberate, circular motion, after which he changed position so that he stood directly opposite Adam. He sat. He waited. He looked with some intensity at the table, shifted his eyes to stare at the ceiling and then at each of the four walls as if he were in deep thought. The other Elders exchanged glances, unclear as to what to say or do. None dared to speak. The ChairAnt finally rested his heavy eyes on Adam. The other Elders followed suit.

Elder AyJay tapped the table with one of his front feet. 'You, Adam Ant, made wild and hysterical claims about what has caused the odour that, by the way, all of us are well aware of, and what has caused the temperature to rise. You have been irresponsible in creating alarm by making the preposterous claim that the change in the weather is due to ant activity. Our subcommittee has examined your irrational notions and dismissed them. There is a pattern in your behaviour, Elder Adam Ant, that has any objective observer concluding you are either irresponsible or unbalanced.

'Regarding your recent reprehensible behaviour, you failed, first of all, to ensure a bee had been killed by your workers prior to having it carried into our metropolis, after which you failed to prevent it escaping. You took it upon yourself to release Pheromones of Utmost Urgency, when procedure specifically states that you are to consult this Council prior to taking such an action. You have been a law unto yourself, Elder Adam Ant. Secondly, you failed to follow the Queen's instructions to abort your surveying of the valley. You are accused of insurbordination, Elder Adam Ant. Do you deny these charges?'

'The forests are dying,' said Adam.

'Do you deny these charges?'

'We must reduce the number of our livestock. We have to arrest the deterioration of the soil. It is we who are responsible for this stifling, terrible odour and the dramatic rise in temperature.'

'Elder Adam! Do you deny these charges?'

'We have to change ant behaviour. We must cease transporting vast amounts of plant matter into our metropolis for processing. The valley will, in a matter of months, become uninhabitable. We have to plant seeds, reduce our population.'

'Elder Adam!'

'Our practice of stripping an entire tree of its foliage to farm fungus on the decomposing leaves has created vast mounds of waste that have generated harmful gases.'

'Do you deny these charges?'

'What if I'm correct? I ask you to consider this one question. You've all heard me issue my warnings. If what I'm saying comes to pass, then none of you will be able to say *I did not know.* You all know. I have told you. I demand to see the Queen and ——'

'I shall ask you one more time, and no more,' said Elder AyJay. 'You have been warned. Answer this question: Did you abort your surveying of the valley?'

Adam looked into the hard, unblinking eyes of each Elder

in turn. 'I don't deny surveying some of The Eternal Valley.'

'Then you are condemned for doing so. I continue. You are responsible for providing food for over thirty million subjects. This is so, is it not?'

'It is so.'

AyJay Heartland leaned back onto his rear legs and pointed his antennae accusingly. 'You departed AntLand without permission. You informed no-one of your impending absence, an absence that you knew, on your departure, would last several months. You did not appoint a second-in-charge to manage your responsibilities, presumably so that your intended escapade remained a secret. Do you deny any of *these* charges? I repeat, Elder Adam, they are charges.'

'I deny none.'

AyJay Heartland rose. 'Then I have no reason to delay sentence. By the authority vested in me by by Her Royal Highness, Queen Ant, our Great Mother, I, AyJay Heartland, ChairAnt of The Council of Elders and the Queen's Senior Advisor, sentence you, Elder Adam Ant to ――'

'I set foot upon The Sacred Circle of Cliffs.'

The Elders, save for AyJay Heartland, gasped as one.

'I climbed The Sacred Circle of Cliffs.'

Eyes widened and antennae stood upright, bristling in confusion and outrage. Some of the Elders, barely able to speak, wrapped their antennae in some peculiar tight embrace around their heads, uttered a cry then began rocking back and forth. Others gnashed their mandibles, looking from one Elder to another for reasons they knew not why.

Amidst the uproar, Adam said: 'I climbed to the top of The Sacred Circle of Cliffs. I was not struck down. There was no thunderbolt from AntGod. There was no rumbling of the ground upon which I walked.'

Several of the Elders twisted their heads, thoraxes, antennae and abdomens in a vain attempt to prevent themselves from hearing such blasphemy. Others moaned out aloud to drown out Adam's words. Several looked upon him with eyes that threatened violent intent.

'After climbing to the top of the cliffs, I descended part of the way down the other side of The Sacred Circle. There's no great darkness. NoWorld is a myth. I've seen. With my own eyes, I've seen.'

'Blasphemer! Impious, irreverent heretic! Eyes that must be plucked from your blasphemous face!' cried Gredo. 'Immediately! Immediately!' He looked towards AyJay Heartland for confirmation of the punishment to be meted out to the heretic. The ChairAnt, however, stood silent and still.

Two Elders had to be restrained from attacking Adam, their mandibles grinding violently in the uproar. Several called for Adam's immediate execution, while others, so stunned at his outrageous words, were unable to react. The disturbance continued unabated. The room filled with shouts and a chaotic turmoil of legs, antennae and mandibles, pheromones flowing in every direction, one of the Elders even letting out an involuntary high-pitched prolonged cackle, so taken was he by the depth of Adam's profanity. In the confused clamour of outrage and threats, Adam knew that at any moment they could set upon him and tear him limb from limb.

As quickly as the noise had erupted, it died. The Elders

stood in various strange postures like a bizarre assembly of statues, mouths agape, antennae erect, eyes transfixed. None looked more astonished than AyJay Heartland.

'Speak, Elder Adam.' It was the Queen. She stood at the threshold of the chamber, Zekiel by her side. She entered, while Zekiel waited outside.

Chapter 13

The Queen Interrogates Adam Ant

'It seems,' said the Queen, 'that what I have been told by my ChairAnt is correct: you are completely insane, Adam Ant. Or perhaps that is not the case? Could it be that you have something of interest to tell us?'

The Elders stood motionless, bewildered as to what to do or say.

'We believe there is a well-known and time-honored procedure required of those in their Queen's presence to show their respect,' she said.

Adam was the first to respond. Upon his initiative, all but AyJay Heartland prostrated themselves before their Queen. The ChairAnt remained standing, his antennae bristling, his eyes darkening. The Queen laid her eyes upon him. She waited. She raised her antennae quizzically. 'Yes, our ChairAnt? We await your response.'

He bowed.

'Inadequate,' the Queen said.

He lowered his head further to the ground. His eyes, Adam saw, were smouldering. Pheromones of outrage seeped from his legs, head and thorax. 'With respect, Your Majesty, for your own protection, you must return to ——'

'No, we shall not return to our Royal Chamber. We would like to hear what Adam Ant has to say. Is there any reason why we should not hear him, my ChairAnt?'

Silence.

'We await your response.'

Adam watched AyJay Heartland intently out of the corners of all his eyes. How was the ChairAnt going to deal with this humiliation? Adam knew that AyJay Heartland had sway over all the Elders, but surely they would side with their Queen if it came to an open disagreement between the two? And what of The Imperial Runners outside The Council Chamber, all personally chosen and trained by AyJay Heartland? Would the ChairAnt dare call upon either the Elders or The Runners to support him were he to defy the Queen? And to support him in doing ... what?

AyJay Heartland took one deep breath, then another, then a third. Oh, dear AntGod, thought Adam, do as your Queen tells you, ChairAnt. Adam had an image of the chaos that would ensue were AyJay Heartland to challenge the Queen's authority.

'No, Your Majesty, there is not.'

A brief audible sigh of relief swept the room, then there was silence except for the sounds of the slight twitchy shuffling of antennae. Adam and the Elders remained prostrated, staring at some spot on the floor, waiting for the Queen's response.

'All rise.'

Nothing like this had ever happened in the history of AntLand.

'Our ChairAnt?'

'Yes, my Queen?'

'Why had we not been informed of Elder Adam's return?'

'You have been of late preoccupied with your princess, Your Majesty, and I did not wish to ——'

'Nonsense. Try again.'

'The Council is meeting to discuss Elder Adam's journey, Your Majesty. I had intended to inform you of his return upon the conclusion of our meeting.'

'Is that so.' She addressed the Councillors 'Take up position around us, in a circle.' She rested her heavy eyes on Adam, looked him up and down then said, 'Continue, Elder Adam. Tell us what you have seen. You were saying that you had seen something with your own eyes. Inform us, please.'

Adam bowed. 'I disobeyed you, my Queen, it is true. But why would I risk my position as an Elder? I had good reason to do so.'

'Elder Adam, we have not asked you a question to have you answer us with a question. We heard you say *I have seen*. What, pray tell, did you see?'

'I could have gone to my grave and not told a soul of what I'd observed, Your Highness. I could, even now, keep to myself what I saw and not take the risk of being condemned for what others would say was my blasphemous behaviour.'

'Enough, Elder Adam. At what point are you going to tell us what you saw?'

After completing his report, the Elders looked to the Queen for guidance as to how to respond. Adam felt their hostility, their incredulity, their disgust. Their antennae quivered in rapid motions of indignation while their bodies became taut in their restrained fury. He knew that if the Queen dismissed all he had said he would be immediately condemned by The Council. His life hung in the balance. All was dependent on her response.

'You have proof, do you not, Elder Adam?'

'I do.'

'You are referring to Zekiel the Wise.'

'Yes, Your Majesty. But I've not told you all. I haven't told you the worst. The alien left me three messages, which I found in my camp. One message was a greeting.'

The Elders looked at each other. AyJay Heartland narrowed his eyes.

'That was one message,' said the Queen. 'What was the second?'

'The second was a request.'

Pause.

'Look at us, Elder Adam. We feel your pheromones of trepidation. Tell us all you know. You said there were three messages.'

'The third was a threat.'

'Assistant-Elder Gredo, summon Zekiel the Wise.'

Adam Ant was escorted into a room off The Council Chamber. An Imperial Runner stood outside as guard. Adam could hear the rumbling of voices and the violent twitching of antennae from the chamber but understood nothing of what was said. Then there was quiet.

Assistant-Elder Gredo entered the room. 'Do you,' he said, 'know the effect of your apocalyptic hysteria? Not one of the Elders believes you. Why the Queen suffers your idiocy is a mystery to us all, but you've been warned: if they have their way you'll be executed for spreading alarm through the empire. Without the Queen's support such would be your fate. Adam Ant, come with me.'

They returned to The Council Chamber.

'We seek answers to several questions, Elder Adam,' said the Queen. 'You must answer briefly. Similar questions will be asked of Zekiel the Wise, who has been taken to another room so that he does not hear your responses. Your answers and his will be compared. Our first question is this: What was the approximate distance in antbody lengths between the nests of the red ants and the black ants?'

Adam replied.

'What was the antbody height of the rock you hid behind when you observed the raid of the red ants?'

Her questioning continued for a great length of time.

'Elder Adam Ant, you are to stand in that corner opposite us where we can see you,' said the Queen. 'You are to close your eyes during the time it takes us to ask of Zekiel the same questions. There is to be no communication between you and Zekiel. You will not speak. You will not look at him. Your antennae are to remain rigid. No pheromones are to be exuded from any part of your body.'

After the Queen had asked Zekiel the same questions, she addressed the Elders. 'Leave us. We wish to be alone with Elder Adam Ant and Zekiel the Wise. Wait for our instructions outside the chamber. We shall summon you if and when we decide you are to return.'

AyJay Heartland turned when he reached the door to give Adam a long, hostile look.

When they were alone, the Queen said, 'Did you find a suitable location for a colony, Elder Adam?'

'No, Your Majesty.'

'Is it because you cut short your surveying because you wanted to warn us of what you saw?'

'Yes, Your Majesty.'

'We have two commands for you. We may not be in a position to repeat what we are about to say. Listen carefully. You are to resume your exploration. We are determined to establish a colony. It is to be a place that has water, is sheltered and is hidden from view. It must be a place that is secure from the heat and this terrible odour. Secondly, there will come a time when we might issue you with instructions that will be confusing for you. You will be perplexed because what we shall instruct you to do will go against your better instincts. But you must obey. You must not question. You must respond immediately to our order. Do you understand?'

'Yes, Your Majesty.'

'It may well concern the Princess.'

'I understand, Your Majesty.'

'Instruct the Elders to return.'

The Council members resumed their positions.

'This is our decision,' the Queen said. 'Elder Adam Ant will depart tomorrow with Zekiel and any assistants they require to fulfil our desire to find a site for ——'

At that moment, the door to The Council Chamber

was thrown open. An Imperial Runner burst in, gasping in spasms. He had a wild look of horror in his eyes. His entire body shook in violent convulsions, his antennae jerking and twisting in confusion. 'Aliens,' he said. 'Alien ants.'

Chapter 14

The Arrival of the Alien Ambassadors

All eyes immediately turned to Adam. 'They are here for a response to their threat!' he said.

'Elder Adam, take charge,' said the Queen.

It was AyJay Heartland, however, who responded. He called for a hundred Imperial Runners to escort the Queen to a safe location. He ordered that all paths leading to the Queen be sealed and pheromones laid as decoys to lead astray any foreign ant that might succeed in gaining entry into the city.

Adam bolted out of The Council Chamber as the Queen was ushered to safety, happening, for the briefest of moments, to cast a glance at AyJay Heartland. Surely, surely that was not an effusion of pleasure he detected emanating from the ChairAnt?

If any confirmation was needed that the Runner's announcement was true, it was provided the moment they exited the pathway leading from The Council Chamber to the city's main thoroughfare: news of the presence of aliens and the detection of their foreign pheromones had spread throughout the metropolis. Some of the subjects of AntLand were thumping the tips of their abdomen on the ground, while others, in the grip of hysteria, compressed their antennae and ran mindlessly here and there, expectorating and nipping at one another, emitting strange sounds and chaotic chemical discharges. Order had completely broken down. With their carers having abandoned them, the aphids and caterpillars trembled in their chambers, fearful for their lives. Livestock were roaming freely, infected by the fear they distinguished in their masters. Adam pushed his way through mobs of distraught ants, many of whom had prostrated themselves and were praying to AntGod.

Adam and Zekiel rushed to the surface, stopping at The Imperial Gate. The ants labouring on The Royal Tower had ceased work. They stood as a silent body looking in the one direction, ten million fear-stunned ants made immobile by the strangest sight they had ever laid eyes on. Behind them was the partially completed tower, its enormous shadow stretching like some accusing claw to where fifty aliens, each different from the other, stood in a line, some 100 antbody lengths from The Imperial Gate. There were red, black and green ants, some the size of the subjects of AntLand, others much larger. One stood at about the height of ten antbodies and was the most fierce-looking creature anyone in AntLand had ever seen. And there, standing amongst them, was the yellow ant. As soon as Adam and Zekiel appeared at the gate, the yellow ant took three steps forward, then stopped.

For several moments Adam did not know what to do.

'He wants to talk,' said Zekiel. 'Take three steps forward, Master.'

AyJay Heartland suddenly appeared. He took hold of one

of Adam's mandibles. 'Stay where you are, Elder Adam.'

'You do not have the Queen's authority. I'm the one she told to take charge. Desist, AyJay Heartland, desist!' Before the ChairAnt had time to reply, Adam had taken three steps towards the aliens.

The alien responded with another ten paces. Eventually the yellow ant and Adam met halfway between The Imperial Gate and the other aliens.

The ChairAnt, to Adam's consternation, had followed him to where he now stood.

The yellow ant spoke. 'I have been chosen as spokes-ant because it was I who made initial contact with you. I come as a friend. Whether I remain your friend depends on your response to what I have to ask of you, which I do on behalf of all those ants you yourself saw after you followed my scent onto the other side of the cliffs. We are well aware of the odours and the deforestation in your valley.' He turned to wave a claw at those who stood behind him. 'We experienced the same problems in our own kingdoms but did not act quickly enough to correct the damage our behaviour had caused. You, however, have time to undo the destruction done to your empire. We know what needs to be done. We can assist you in protecting your city. But you must also assist us. You are our only hope for survival. We are here as ambassadors of each of our species. We are here to receive your response.'

'What is your request?' AyJay Heartland said.

'ChairAnt,' Adam said. 'I shall do the negotiating.'

'We are starving,' said the yellow ant. 'Our ants are dying in great numbers every day. We have been reduced to desperate measures to stay alive. I urge you to assist us with food so that we can assist you.'

AyJay Heartland spoke. 'Elder Adam has informed us of what he has seen. You ants fight amongst yourselves. You eat one another.'

'AyJay Heartland, you must leave negotiations to me!'

The ChairAnt ignored him. 'You behave as barbarians. And you expect us to help you? You think you are a threat to us? I speak on behalf of Her Majesty, Queen Ant, and The Council of Elders. Your request for food is denied.'

'You do not speak for the Queen, Elder AyJay!' said Adam.

'Oh, please ... What was the word you used? Desist. *You* are the one who must desist, young Adam. You see, I *do* speak for the Queen. You saw me as you left The Council Chamber. You detected my pheromones. My Imperial Runners, those Runners you instructed to escort Her Majesty to a safe location? Yes, Adam Ant, *my* Runners have returned her to *my* safe location.'

'Elder AyJay, everyone heard the Queen tell me to take charge!'

'You have overestimated yourself and underestimated me, Adam Ant.' He turned to the yellow ant. 'Do not think this disagreement between this young ant and myself betokens weakness. You say you can assist us in managing our empire. We do not require the assistance of barbarians. We want no contact with our inferiors. You are, I presume, not only asking me to feed you from our reserve supplies but are also, AntGod forbid, seeking my permission to settle in our valley. Your requests are denied.'

'AyJay Heartland! No!'

'No? No, you say, Adam Ant?' He snapped his mandibles. Two Imperial Runners, standing at attention at The Imperial Gate, broke into a run. They restrained Adam by taking hold of his legs then twisted his antennae so that intelligible communication with the alien was not possible. The worker ants gasped to see Elder Adam treated with such disrespect.

AyJay returned to the alien. 'You must not listen to the rantings of this youngster. You have been misled by him. He speaks for no-one. He carries no authority. I am the ant with whom you must deal. So that there is no misunderstanding, take note. You dare threaten us if we do not assist you? You dare threaten war? Your threat does not frighten me. A bee, it seems, has informed you of the wealth of our supplies. If that is so, then what that bee has told you is, indeed, true. We are organised. We are strong. We are determined. We are an empire of thirty million. You are weak. Leave the valley immediately. Do not return to our empire in the misguided hope that there will be further negotiations. Let me speak once again plainly: if you return you will be met with violence.'

'You have,' said the yellow ant, 'perhaps not understood the seriousness of our situation. We are desperate. Therefore to survive we will be forced to take desperate measures.'

'I will not deplete our resources for you. Your desperate straits are not my concern. They are the consequence of your incompetence and inferiority and barbarity. Depart.' He snapped his mandibles again. Several Imperial Runners responded. 'Escort these cannibals from our empire. If they resist, employ as many other Runners as required to expel them.' He summoned Zekiel. 'Do you feel any affection for Elder Adam?'

'None, Master.'

'During your journey together, were any bonds of friendship created between you and this traitor?'

'None, Master.'

'Are you loyal to AntLand?'

'Yes, Master.'

'Are you loyal to our Queen?'

'Yes, Master.'

'Then show that you are loyal to her ChairAnt by removing this traitorous Elder from my sight.'

AyJay turned his back on the aliens and began walking to The Imperial Gate. As Adam was being led away he called after the ChairAnt. 'Elder AyJay! We have no choice. We must share, if only to avoid conflict. You don't have the authority to make such a decision. Their demands have to be taken to the Queen, to The Council.'

AyJay Heartland marched directly to his workers and communicated to them the alien's demands and what he referred to as his heroic response, after which he asked them to contrast his decisive and fearless reaction to that of Adam Ant who, he said, was a shameful placater, a weak appeaser, one who had betrayed – yes, betrayed! – AntLand by succumbing to the alien's threats and agreed, without the authority of The Council or their Queen, to share with aliens – *aliens!* – their reserve supplies of food.

'Was my daring, valiant response one that meets with your approval?' he asked.

'Yes, ChairAnt!'

'Is it commensurate with the heroic actions of our forebears?'

'Yes, ChairAnt!'

'Do you think I could ever betray you?'

'No!'

'Or our empire?'

'No!'

'Or our Queen?'

'Never!'

'Are you as proud of me as I am of you?'

'Yes, ChairAnt!'

'Then rejoice.'

The response of AyJay's workers was echoed by those within the city. Their rousing cry shook the very foundations of The Royal Tower.

'Ant-Land! Ant-Land! Ant-Land! Ay-Jay! Ay-Jay! Ay-Jay!'

The ChairAnt strutted proudly through The Imperial Gate. This was, many were to later say, AntLand's proudest moment.

'Come Master, I am to take you to where you are to be detained.'

Adam turned to look at the aliens who had begun their long journey back to the cliffs. 'Oh, dear AntGod, save us from ourselves.'

Zekiel touched Adam's mandible with one of his own. He inclined his head to make contact with that of his master. 'Shall we go to your cell?'

Upon arrival at the entry to the metropolis, Adam said, 'Where will this end, Zekiel?'

'The ants we saw, Master, when we were on The Sacred Circle of Cliffs, left their homelands for a purpose – to save themselves. There is the possibilty that there are more of their species who have yet to arrive, and many other species, as well. What we have seen could be just the beginning. If I am correct, then we need to prepare for the arrival of many, many more aliens.'

'With the Queen also confined, Zekiel, who is there with authority to save us?'

'Each one of us, Master, has within him ancestral and successional longings. We must obey that for which we, the dead and the unborn, yearn.'

'Whose longings? Whose yearning?'

'To respond, feeling the weight of expectations. All expectations, Master. Our response is all. One must feel melancholy eyes watching, waiting. He who is able, must act to fulfil the dreams of those who came before and those who are yet to come. Inherited hunger speaks the truth. We must bear witness through the eyes of those whom we serve, Master.'

'And so?'

'And so. Whatever the consequences.'

'Zekiel! Please!'

'Come, Master.'

As Zekiel led Adam through the gate, they felt the ground tremble with the cries of the ants. 'Best! Best! Best!'

AntLand's refrain continued well into the night. While the Queen, anticipating Adam's fate, released the most potent, inviolable and sacrosanct of all emissions – a Royal Pheromonic Pardon – ensuring that it was communicated immediately, ant to ant throughout the entire empire.

Over the following two days, Zekiel anonymously released pheromones of his own, informing AntLanders that the rising temperature and the odious gas were due to ant activity, and that the only way to deal with the enemy was, in fact, not to engage him in combat, but rather to befriend him. He proposed that there was only one way to avoid war, and that was to share their reserves of food. So that his message could not be traced back to him, he corrupted his pheromones with caterpillar, greenfly and snail urine and excrement, the rotting carcasses of a bee, two butterflies, three ladybirds and several worker ants, and the sticky honeydew from several aphids.

The Council of Elders held an emergency meeting in response, after which a stream of pheromones of their own were emitted, accusing this *cowardly, secretive snake*, this anonymous *heretical apostate* of being an *incognito alarmist*, a *shadowy warmist*, a *faceless green fascismo* and, worst of all, a supporter of Adam Ant who, they said, had disobeyed the Queen and was now undermining the empire's preparation for war.

The actions of this *collaborator* necessitated, AyJay Heartland announced, the immediate imposition of a State of Emergency: clearly, AntLand had traitors in its midst. Mighty rewards were offered to any ant who could reveal the identity of the turncoat who had continued releasing pheromones of false information designed, no doubt, to destabilise the empire, as well as the identities of those who either actively campaigned with that viper or offered him refuge. The true believers, AyJay Heartland said, those whom he now referred to as *patriotic refusants*, would hunt down this renegade and every ant who was his disciple, patron or adherent. They, the loyal, devoted ones, had faith in their leader and the empire's ability to squash any rebellion from within as well as defeat any cannibalistic group of savages foolish enough to attack their mighty empire.

After another emergency meeting, The Council of Elders announced that AyJay Heartland would assume sole control of the empire until the present crisis passed. The title conferred upon him was Dear Leader. Curfews and a law banning the criticism of AyJay Heartland were imposed by decree. A large, select group of Imperial Runners was created with the sole objective of hunting down the ant who was spreading what The Council said was malevolent information.

Two days later, Elder Adam was summoned to appear before a newly appointed Discipline Committee chaired by Assistant-Elder Gredo. Adam was accused of spreading wicked and pre-meditated rumours, a crime which, according to Gredo, undermined morale.

'You know very well,' said Gredo, 'that we could face an attack any day now from those aliens.'

'And you know that it was not I who spread those rumours.'

'And yet,' said Gredo, ignoring Adam's reply, 'you have, with a malicious intent, distracted us from our preparations.'

'Our Queen pardoned me.'

'Exactly! And why would she pardon you if there was nothing you have done to pardon?'

'Show me proof that it was I who authored those rumours.'

'Shame on you, Adam Ant! You ask for proof? Here's my response: You have the opportunity to recant your destructive notions as well as those of your supporters, join the growing body of *refusants* who deny that the cause in the change in the weather pattern is antmade, and assist the empire in preparing for war. Will you humble yourself before The Council and recant? Yes or no?'

'No.'

'Imperial Guard! Return this ant to his cell.'

Chapter 15

Zekiel's Double Game

In the weeks that followed, AntLand's Dear Leader emitted pheromonic bulletins of his own that, distributed to every ant in the empire, were designed to bolster confidence and keep order. Ants coming from The NoWorld, he said, were agents of darkness. They were lowly creatures, indicated as such by their colour. The superior ant was he who was entirely black, not the bizarre yellow, the repugnant green and the comical red of the enemy. AntGod Himself was black, as everyone knew. They, the subjects of AntLand, were AntGod's Chosen, and with AntGod on their side, they would prevail over these heathen creatures who worshipped strange gods and practised cannibalism. Indeed, it was their duty as AntLanders to rid the universe of this vermin. AyJay Heartland insisted that their best form of defence was to strengthen determination and hope, that no coalition of disparate ants could match the organisational finesse of AntLand: this ragbag collection of non-believers would soon descend into chaos, he said; no gathering of pagan ants thrown together in haste after having been at war with each other could maintain discipline. It was imperative, therefore, that work on The Royal Tower continue: this display of confidence would strike fear in the heart of the enemy should they even consider carrying out their threats. 'And were these aliens to do the impossible and find the means of crossing The Eternal Plains without our knowing,' AyJay Heartland announced, 'how could they even enter the city? Now that our vents have been closed off for reasons of security, there is a single exit and entry point, one we can maintain with vast numbers. It was for this reason that I insisted, many months ago, that the city have only one point of entry and departure: The Imperial Gate.'

No-one could remember him ever saying such a thing, but it had to be true because AyJay, the ants knew, would not lie.

The work on the tower continued but was slowed down by the ghastly odour that, on some days, exhibited a taut orange oppressiveness that claimed many lives. Work was also delayed by the weather: nights of frost were followed by brief but violent periods of rainfall or hail storms.

The erratic weather affected not only the amount of honeydew produced by the aphids and caterpillars, but also the rate of growth of the livestock AntLand kept for its supply of meat. The Dear Leader announced a reduction in rations for all subjects. Face masks were distributed to every ant labouring on the tower and their usage made compulsory.

Zekiel requested an urgent audience with AyJay Heartland.

'Those ants who once worked under the former Elder's supervision when he was The Royal Forager and Grand Protector of Food Supplies still speak fondly of him,' Zekiel said.

'But they have been informed of his treachery!'

'His seed-harvesters, resin collectors, scouts and foragers find it hard to believe that the traitor has betrayed AntLand.'

'Then I shall release more bulletins.'

'Many saw him throw himself into the mouth of the bee-scout, Dear Leader. Many still refer to him as a hero.'

'You correct their attitude?'

'I attempt to do so, but I fear I have not succeeded.'

'You asked for an audience to inform me of this?'

'I have sought an audience to suggest a remedy to counter the positive opinion of Adam Ant and to increase the respect they have of yourself.'

'Speak, Zekiel the Wise.'

Zekiel suggested the creation of a committee comprised of individuals representing every class of ant in the empire. 'May I suggest it be named The Dear Leader's Intercaste Panel? Under my supervision these committee members will investigate and, as a result, gather the necessary evidence to debunk the traitor's views regarding the level of water in the lowest chambers of the metropolis, the temperature and the growing intensity of the odour. I would ensure the collection of the ... How shall I put it? ... the right sort of information.'

The depiction of reason, Zekiel said, would be a powerful weapon to counter this traitor's insidious influence.

'Proceed. Keep me regularly informed.'

'Yes, Dear Leader. May I also suggest I speak to the traitor? Executing him would be the most desirable action to take if it were not for the Queen's pardon and the loyalty of his workers. They respect him. If the aliens attack us, we shall need them to fight. Were we to dispatch the traitor, who knows whether they would defend AntLand with the enthusiasm we shall require? And as for the Queen, it is clear that she is deluded in her favourable opinion of the traitor. But if we are at war, we shall also need her support. In time, she will see through the façade Adam Ant presents to the world and thus see the error of her ways. I advise caution, Dear Leader. I believe I might be able to have him recant. Please forgive my impertinence if I am speaking above my station. I shall be guided by your wisdom.'

'Who will rid me of this meddling ant! He is a running sore on the body politic, Zekiel, a lightning rod for those who might be discontented. I know! Oh, yes, I am well aware that there are those amongst us who pity him. How I long to dispatch the renegade. And yet, to remove him would, as you say, create other problems. Do what you can.'

'There was,' said Zekiel to Adam, 'a time when the old, wise ants spoke out against AyJay Heartland. Now I am the last of that generation. He waited until they had all died before making plain what you and I now know to have been his long-held schemes. Our survival is at stake. Long and hard have I prayed to AntGod for guidance as to what I should do to save you, to save our empire; and late last night, not long before dawn, I believe He answered me. It was not in divine pheromones but in the whispering of the wind and the sudden change in the moonlight. I felt and sensed a great foreboding, Master, but also the flimsiest, most fragile of hopes. There will be great losses such as we have never experienced, but we shall survive. I had confirmation last night. There will be sacrifice and there will be salvation. I ask for your blessing.'

'Oh, Zekiel,' said Adam, 'it is you who should bless me. Before you depart this abominable place, let us bless one another.'

And so, on the same hour every day, Zekiel took with him AntLand's Intercaste Panel, a group comprising sanitation workers, foragers, hunters, scouts and nursemaids, amongst whom was Nano. And to ensure his panel was truly representative, he also appointed mealy bugs, aphids, sapsucking insects and caterpillars. The facts and figures relating to the rising level of water and temperature and the increasing toxicity of the odour were implanted in their minds.

And still the subjects of AntLand sweltered. Antennae and face masks hung drooping. Some blamed the frenetic activity of the millions of ants labouring on the tower for the heatwave and the terrible smell in the city. Frequent rousing bulletins were made to ensure the workers completed the tower by the time of the empire's anniversary celebrations.

Two months after the appearance of the aliens, Zekiel, having being promoted to Adam's role as The Royal Forager and Grand Protector of Food Supplies, led AntLand's thousands of hunters out of the city for their regular harvest of insects. They were greeted by an enormous billboard, much larger than the other signs, designed to intimidate enemy scouts.

The Universe has a New Centre.
Look upon our Tower, oh ye fools,
And Despair.

Zekiel's hunters returned with their lowest ever yield: the constant heat was sucking the moisture out of the soil, and with the fewer plants in the diminishing forests there were fewer insects. But one particular butterfly was fortunate to have had Zekiel nearby when dozens of ants fell upon it; fortunate for the empire, too, because just as the ants were about to deliver their death stings, the butterfly let out a mighty scream, pleading for the sparing of its life for information vital to AntLand.

Zekiel reported the butterfly's information to Adam. 'The butterfly informed me that alien ants, Master, have overcome all their differences and have created a Coalition of the Willing. They are practising military manoeuvres every day. Of greater concern is what is occurring far, far away, many months travel by foot or by wing beyond where the aliens have established their camp. This butterfly told me millions of ants are fleeing failed cities and empires and are making their way to AntLand. He told me of valleys too numerous to count that have suffered from plant-withering heat waves, drought and fires, of melting snow forcing untold numbers of ants to migrate.'

'It is as I feared,' said Adam. 'Secure this insect, Zekiel. Do you have authority to inspect the construction of The Royal Tower?'

'Yes, Master, but only from the outside. I am not permitted to enter it.'

'Then scale its external wall. Climb to its highest point. I fear what you will discover. Return quickly.'

As he climbed, Zekiel noted that the ants working on the tower had used a mixture of clay, sand, sticks and seeds to enclose all the openings to the ventilation shafts. He enquired as to why they were making inoperable the tower's cooling system. None knew. They were simply doing as they had been told.

'By whom?' he asked.

'The Dear Leader,' they said.

He climbed as far as he could and, squinting in the glare of a pale sky, saw that the snowline on The Sacred Circle had dramatically receded. Perhaps, he thought, the butterfly had flown over The Sacred Circle and seen for itself the extent of the melting snow. He went down to the prison in which he had placed him. The butterfly was dead.

'He did not die by natural causes, Master. His neatly-arranged dismembered parts lay on the ground.'

'He was murdered?'

'Yes, his body parts were displayed in a manner that made clear he had died a violent death. I believe it serves as some warning. But killed by whom? And a warning to whom?'

'AyJay Heartland?' said Adam.

'No, Master. The odour and hunger pheromonic signals and odour trails I detected on and around the butterfly are not those of our ants.'

'What? An alien has gained entry into the metropolis? But … but the vents have been closed. How could they enter through The Imperial Gate?'

'I do not know. But what other conclusion are we to

make? Unless, of course, the butterfly had had contact with the aliens and had brought those pheromonic signals into our metropolis on its own body.'

'Perhaps. What of the odour, Zekiel? What of the temperature in our metropolis?'

'The weather is unpredictable, Master. Despite the rising temperature, we have had much rainfall, as you know. The clay floors of our passages and thoroughfares have become sodden, preventing the odour from escaping. Tell me, Master, are you being fed well?'

'Well enough.'

'Come, Master.'

Adam Ant unfurled his tongue and Zekiel regurgitated liquid into his mouth.

Proof of the danger to AntLand came, however, in a completely unexpected form. Zekiel was making his weekly reading of the water level, accompanied by The Intercaste Panel, when they heard, from within the wall behind them, a sound, a scratching noise, of some creature digging. They exchanged a look; no-one spoke. They crept to a corner from where they could watch, unobserved. Their worst fears were confirmed when grains of sand came crashing down only a few antbodies away from them, revealing a tunnel. Two antennae protruded from the opening – green antennae. An alien's head poked out of the opening. The alien saw Zekiel and, in a panicked frenzy, emitted a cloud of alarmed pheromones. The stimulant, spurting out of his body and into the thoroughfare, aroused panic amongst the members of The Intercaste Panel, giving those aliens behind the green ant time to retreat. It took a few moments for Zekiel and his panellists to respond. Zekiel leapt out of their corner and, throwing himself into the tunnel, seized the spy. They heard the cries of the other aliens retreating into the depths of the passage they had excavated. Imperial Runners were summoned, but they arrived too late. All but the one alien had escaped down the tunnel which, an investigation was to reveal, stretched for thousands of antbody lengths towards The Sacred Circle.

The green ant was interrogated by AyJay Heartland himself at a specially-convened meeting of the Elders. AyJay told him his life would be spared if he responded truthfully to his questions. The alien told of the species that had recently joined their ranks, which consisted of millions of fire ants and thousands of queens. He told him of other species that had standing armies of nomads who were becoming increasingly impatient and wanted to bring forward the date of the invasion. He said the attack was to occur in four months' time, which, by chance, coincided with the anniversary of AntLand's founding. Once AyJay had the information he required, he had the alien decapitated.

The tunnel the aliens had created was filled in. AyJay Heartland began immediate plans to strengthen the security of the metropolis.

The following morning, one of Zekiel's ants released the preliminary findings of The Dear Leader's Intercaste Panel. Olfactory messages passed from one ant to the next in rapid succession, the alarming news streaming through passages, galleries and storage rooms, into the farmlands and the nurseries, to the disposal sites and cemeteries, even to the foraging hunters. Panic gripped the metropolis.

The ant who released these findings was Nano.

Chapter 16

The Reign of Terror Begins

Late that same morning, an Imperial Runner reported a disturbing find to The Dear Leader. AyJay Heartland broke off from a meeting with Zekiel during which they had been discussing the release of these findings. He strode through AntLand's main thoroughfare, flanked by several Imperial Runners, who escorted him to The Imperial Gate. He stopped. He stood fuming before the signs at the building site, twitching his antennae with agitation. Someone had sprayed them with pheromonic graffiti. On one sign was written: *Our Current Status: UnChosen and Lied To.* Whoever had committed this abomination was questioning the references to AntLanders being the children of AntGod. AyJay Heartland then examined the billboard on which was written the proclamation celebrating the tower as their *glory in the glorious history of AntLand*. Over this sign was sprayed another outrage: *The Sacred Circle of Cliffs is an Unglorious Deceit.* The graffiti on the third sign spoke directly to the aliens' despair and challenged AyJay Heartland's authority: *Look upon AyJay's Folly and Laugh. We share resources or we die. All ants are AntLanders.* On the ground, The Imperial

Gate, the walls of the city's main thoroughfares and in many of the chambers were provocative pheromones ridiculing The Dear Leader.

AyJay Heartland had the pheromones scanned by Imperial Runners. Readings were made and memorised. Once the graffiti was removed, AyJay announced that an Extraordinary Assembly of All Subjects of AntLand would be held immediately in The Grand Hall. Those unable to gain entry into the hall were to assemble in the main thoroughfare and those passages, vaults and chambers closest to the hall. Attendance by every AntLander except Adam Ant and his guard (and, of course, the Queen) was made compulsory.

Thirty million ants made their way to the specified assembly points. The Elders sat on the platform just as they had done for the Queen's address some nine months previously. A vast congregation waited in anticipation as one hour passed, a second ... Deliberately late, thought Zekiel, who had been allocated what had previously been Adam's position.

Three hours after they had taken their places, thousands of Imperial Runners suddenly emerged in military formation from an antechamber to the side of the platform. AntLand had so many Runners? Zekiel was alarmed. Why? When? How? The entire gathering, including all the Elders, gasped in amazement and horror, mightily impressed but equally bewildered and frightened by the display of power. What was this? thought Zekiel. An army? AntLand did not have an army, AntLand had never had an army. Where had these Imperial Runners come from? Where were they trained? How were they kept from view?

The Runners made their way methodically towards the rear, scrutinising with their antennae each of those ants seated in the hall. Adam saw one Runner pause, run his antennae repeatedly over the head, thorax and abdomen of one of the assembled ants then, after calling for assistance from another Runner, grasp the ant firmly by the legs and drag him to the side. Thrown to the ground, the ant remained largely out of view.

Elder Gredo, recently promoted from his previous position as an assistant, approached the middle of the platform. In the name of The Dear Leader he demanded silence. The terrified assembly obeyed. He commanded that all ants face the front of The Great Hall. Once they had turned their faces to him rather than the Imperial Runners or the apprehended worker, he proclaimed in a booming voice that The Dear Leader was about to enter, and that upon his appearance all his subjects, including his Elders, should bow their heads. As if on cue, a deafening roar from the rear of the hall announced the arrival of AyJay Heartland, ChairAnt of The Council of Elders, Her Majesty's Senior Advisor and AntLand's recently-anointed Dear Leader. Hundreds of Imperial Runners, continuing their thunderous acclamation, fell into two lines, creating a path for AyJay Heartland, who appeared wearing a long, regal, multi-coloured cloak of braided strands of fungi, glued together with honeydew. He walked methodically and stiff-legged, several steps behind the Runners, looking straight ahead as ants craned their heads to gain a view of him.

He slowly mounted the platform. He gestured with the wave of one antenna that the Elders should lift their heads. He turned to face the assembly. He waited until there was not a single movement in the vast sea of subjects before him, then said: 'Raise your heads.'

Imperial Runners stood at attention at the front, rear and to the sides of The Grand Hall. They moved their sharpened mandibles in time. A great unease took hold of the assembly. Too late, too late: Zekiel had long suspected AyJay Heartland's ambitions, but this?

'My fellow AntLanders,' AyJay Heartland began, 'in two months The Royal Tower will be completed, four weeks ahead of time. It stands as a monument to our engineering finesse, its appearance and size a reflection of our intelligence and power. Some time in the near future we shall, in all likelihood, face a horde of barbarians intent on taking by force all that we have created. Our military planning has already begun.

'Do not be alarmed by the presence of so many Imperial Runners. You have nothing to fear while you remain obedient and obey all instructions. Many of you saw the enemy when they intruded upon our empire to make demands. You understand their intent. We shall meet force with force. They will be confronted by overwhelming power and spectacular displays of might. *Shock and awe* are the words which will inspire these Imperial Runners, whose sole purpose is to protect you. Be comforted by their presence.

'To defend our civilisation I have decided that two rings of defensive walls will be built around the tower and The Imperial Gate. The inner ring will rise above the outer so that should the unlikely occur and the enemy is able to breach our first line of defence, he will be struck down in that area between the walls. Each of these two walls will be surmounted by walkways that will enable our defenders to hurl objects at the attackers below.

'We will also construct a water-filled moat, thirty antbodies deep and sixty across, which will surround the outer wall. Anyone foolish enough to attempt swimming across the moat will be a vulnerable target for those defending our metropolis from the outer walkway. No enemy will be able to even approach the first of our walls using their bodies as scaling ladders. No enemy, of course, will be able to dig under such a moat, let alone excavate under the foundations of our concentric walls. We will, therefore, be secure against these uncivilised infidels because the height of the innermost wall will make it impossible for them to scale it. I say that again: it will not be possible for any creature to scale our innermost wall.

'Repeat after me: Shock and awe.'

Millions of voices cried hesitantly as one. 'Shock and awe.'

'Look upon my Imperial Runners, my fellow AntLanders. They have been bred to protect you. They have been trained to fight to the death in your defence, in defence of our empire and your Queen. In your response I detected a lack of enthusiasm. Have faith in them. Have faith in your Dear Leader. Repeat once more after me: Shock and awe!'

'Shock and awe!'

'Louder!'

'Shock and awe!'

'Again! Thrice!'

'Shock and awe! Shock and awe! Shock and awe!'

'Silence. I continue. It will not be possible, I say, for the enemy to scale that wall because we shall stand together, thorax to thorax, abdomen to abdomen, united, loyal, obedient. United in purpose. Loyal to our Queen. Obedient to our Commandments and your Dear Leader.

'Let us, therefore, turn our attention to those who would weaken us from within. You will recall that when our Queen addressed us in this same Grand Hall so few months ago, she said, and I quote: "Ever since the temperature began to rise, the number of eggs we have been producing has increased." She then posed the question: "Why is this so?" Do you, my fellow AntLanders, recall the response she gave to her own question? She said, and I quote: "We do not know. We do not ask. AntGod has willed it so." But now *you* know why. The increase in offspring has given us the opportunity to create this army of Imperial Runners, one small contingent of which you see before you. Yes, my subjects, our Queen responded to AntGod's unspoken command and gifted us the means by which I have built an army, in training at this very moment in the many chambers and passageways and vaults of that part of The Royal Tower which has been completed. Our Queen also said that such an ever-increasing number of offspring is "a sign". She, our only conduit to the divine, informed us that AntGod has instructed us – and, once again, I quote – "to grow in a way that will bring us greater glory". She told us that "It is our destiny that we become bigger, better, best". Repeat!'

The Grand Hall shuddered with the response.

He raised an antenna. The hall fell silent. 'However, we have in our midst traitorous individuals who have been undermining our empire. One member of the so-called

Intercaste Panel has released false information. I have decided, therefore, with the Queen's support, to disband this committee.' He fell silent. He turned to stare hard at Zekiel and cocked his head to one side, frowning, his antennae quivering in restrained fury, wild and violent pheromones streaming onto the platform. 'It will,' he continued, still glaring at Zekiel, 'no longer investigate those features of our empire when the only consequence of a member of that committee's actions has been to weaken us by spreading false information regarding the health of our empire.'

He then turned to face the assembly.

'We also have amidst us a traitor who has been challenging our Queen, our Mother, AntGod's appointed sovereign, our founder, our life-force, without whom we would not exist. This ant, whom we can all see struggling futilely at the side of this great Royal Hall, clearly had a malicious intent. It is he who has been spraying graffiti on our Royal Billboards, challenging the authority of your Dear Leader, making a mockery of your achievement in constructing The Royal Tower.'

He gave a signal to the Runners who had this worker pinned to the ground.

'I regret to have to tell you that this ant has undermined the authority upon which our empire depends, and even questioned the commandments of The Holy AntBook by spraying blasphemous graffiti on our signs and posters and billboards. He threatens the very existence of AntLand with his prophanities, and this we cannot tolerate, as he has even questioned ...' His voice trailed to a whisper; he paused for a long time before his words rose in inflection and volume. 'He has even questioned the very existence of AntGod! Imperial Runners – bring him forth!'

Four Runners dragged their victim towards AyJay Heartland. Zekiel trembled, knowing full well the appalling, harrowing scene they were all about to witness. He felt for the wretched, foolhardy, brave ant. What heroics, he thought, to have taken such risks. And then the old ant realised. He had been told only moments prior to AyJay Heartland's entry into The Grand Hall that one of the pheromonic messages this young ant had sprayed onto one of the signs on The Royal Tower was *The Sacred Circle is an Unglorious Deceit*. Zekiel began to violently shake. Pheromones communicating distress exuding from his legs and head were so powerful that AyJay Heartland turned to look at him. Who else, thought Zekiel, could have written such a thing? Who else would have known? The culprit was Nano.

Zekiel looked on in horror at the fearless young ant, who was avoiding looking into the old ant's eyes so as not to implicate him, was dragged to the front of the hall. *Look at me, Nano. See the admiration in my eyes. I see you, young Nano, I know you as that noble, questioning, bold, curious paragon. What did you say to Adam when he said you exhaust him? That you exhaust yourself? Oh, Nano, nooo ...*

'This ant's pheromones,' said AyJay Heartland, 'match the sacriligeous graffiti sprayed upon the signs celebrating our construction of The Royal Tower.'

Nano was held hard to the ground by one Runner, while another stood over him, his mandibles opening and closing, waiting for a sign from The Dear Leader.

'In these dangerous times there can be no disobedience. Traitors cannot, will not be tolerated. Imperial Runners – do your terrible duty.'

The Runners dragged Nano up onto the platform where an executioner with huge mandibles was waiting for him. The executioner snapped off, one by one, Nano's feet and antennae.

Zekiel shut his eyes and closed his mind to Nano's screams, hearing instead what Nano had once said: *I knew that when Her Majesty informed us of your mission, I felt that she was talking to all of us, yes, but also directly to me, and that I had to join you, to help you. My prayers have been answered. You are doing AntGod's work, Master Adam ...*

Elder Gredo commanded all to stand erect on their rear legs. Zekiel opened his eyes, only to see Nano's head held aloft on a twig.

You asked us once, Nano, if we are civilised ants.

AyJay Heartland stepped down from the platform and slowly departed through the deathly silence of The Grand Hall, flanked again by two rows of Imperial Runners. As The Dear Leader made his way to the rear of The Grand Hall, Elder Gredo announced that martial law would be imposed, effective immediately, to be revoked only when the threat from the aliens had passed.

The following morning Zekiel was summoned to The War Rooms, a labyrinthine section deep in the heart of the city where hundreds of Imperial Runners in full military regalia were coming and going. One of the Runners escorted Zekiel to the entry of AyJay Heartland's Inner Sanctum. Elder

Gredo stood waiting to instruct Zekiel of recently instituted protocols regarding the behaviour of AntLand's subjects when in the presence of The Dear Leader.

'Henceforth, when attending a meeting with our Dear Leader, you are not to look directly into his eyes,' he said.

'Not look into his eyes?'

'Yes.'

'Why?'

'Out of respect, of course. I need to know that you understand. Do you?'

'Yes.'

'And when you are dismissed, walk backwards towards the exit. Do not show disrespect by turning your back on our Dear Leader. Now, wait here. Stand at attention. You will be summoned in time.'

Elder Gredo entered the Inner Sanctum. Zekiel stood rigidly at attention, observed for the entire lengthy period of time by several Imperial Runners who, Zekiel assumed, were AyJay Heartland's personal security guards.

Elder Gredo reappeared. 'The Dear Leader will see you now.'

Zekiel followed Elder Gredo into the Inner Sanctum. The Dear Leader sat behind an enormous slab of wood, staring at a range of maps and lists. Behind him, mounted caterpillar, bee and bird heads hung from the wall.

Zekiel was startled by Elder Gredo's loud exclamation. 'We raise our voices in unison to salute The Dear Leader! We offer you our salutation: Long live our Dear Leader! Old ant, repeat with me this salutation!' Zekiel then cried with Elder

Gredo: 'Long live our Dear Leader!'

Ayjay Heartland continued examining the maps and lists. After several minutes, he looked up.

Zekiel was instructed by Gredo to take two steps towards the slab of wood and to stand directly opposite AyJay Heartland. Elder Gredo then stood to one side.

AyJay Heartland rested his heavy eyes on Zekiel, his face an unfathomable shadow. He stroked the side of his head with one of his antennae. He made as if he was about to speak, hesitated, fell silent then continued his steady, unblinking consideration of Zekiel. 'Look at me.' Zekiel looked up. AyJay Heartland waited until Zekiel was unable to hold his gaze, at which point he said: 'You permitted this executed ant to release false findings. It was he, you see, who also desecrated our billboards.'

'No, Dear Leader.'

'I did not ask you a question. I was making a statement. I did not permit you to contradict me.' His voice, the movement of his antennae and his seeping pheromones diffused savagery.

'If I may speak, Dear Leader.'

'No, you may not. *You* sought the creation of this committee. *You* had full responsibility for the behaviour of those in your charge. I take it you do not agree with the findings of this preliminary report. You may answer.'

'I do not.'

'How is it that such findings were made? You may answer.'

'Such findings were not arrived at by the committee. The executed ant acted alone.'

'Did he.' It was a statement, not a question.

'Yes, he ——'

'What, pray tell, *are* your findings thus far? You may answer.'

'My findings indicate that the changes we are witnessing are consistent with historical changes over time. We have seen them before. We shall see them again.'

'I see. They are not due to our ant activity? You may answer.'

'No.'

'Are you certain? Answer.'

'Yes, I am certain, Dear Leader.'

AyJay Heartland tapped the table with one of his antenna. 'I see.' AyJay Heartland's cold accusing eyes slowly examined Zekiel from his feet to his head. 'I see,' he said again. He turned to Gredo. 'I am wondering whether I might seek the opinion of one of my Runners.'

'Yes, Dear ——'

'If you had listened to my tone, Gredo, you would have realised that I was not asking you a question. My thought was directed to myself.'

'Forgive me, but ——'

'Silence.'

Gredo shut his eyes and folded his antennae.

'Approach, Elder Gredo.'

Gredo stood before AyJay Heartland. He stared at the ground. He was trembling.

AyJay Heartland placed one of his claws under Gredo's jaw and slowly lifted his head. 'Open your eyes.'

Gredo did as he had been commanded.

'Elder Gredo?'

Gredo stood, shaking.

'My tone, you fool. My tone. Elder Gre-*do*? Do you not detect the rising inflection in my voice?'

'Yes, Dear Leader?'

'Instruct one of my Imperial Runners to come immediately.'

When the Runner entered, AyJay Heartland said to him: 'I am wondering whether I can trust this old ant.' He pointed one of his antennae at Zekiel. 'What is your opinion, soldier?'

'I am not qualified to say, Dear Leader.'

'You have nothing to say?'

'Dear Leader, I exist to carry out your instructions. It does not fall to me to have opinions.'

'Ah, do you see, Gredo, what a clever response that is. I trust, Gredo, that you took note of my tone and the flat pitch of my delivery. And took note, too, that what I just said was not a question.' He dismissed the Runner and leaned back on his rear feet, looking at Zekiel. He waited a long time. 'Approach me, old ant. Closer. Closer still. There. Stand still.' He scanned Zekiel's antennae, mandibles, legs, head, thorax and abdomen with both antennae. He leaned on his back legs again and waited. He seemed to be thinking. 'Raise your head. Look at me. Look into my eyes.' He bent forward and slowly scanned, at first, Zekiel's entire exoskeleton, then stared hard into Zekiel's six eyes, one after the other. 'The fondness our subjects have for you might well be warranted. I want to trust you. I wonder, however, whether I *should* trust you. I am no longer so sure. Therefore, you will no longer attend Council meetings. Therefore you must not visit the traitor. You will, however, be given tasks that will enable you to show your worth. You will, therefore, be retaining certain responsibilities. I shall be watching you carefully, old ant. Anyone claiming that the changes in the weather are due to ant activity will encounter swift retribution. Take care. I am assuming you take my meaning. You are silent. Do you see, Gredo, how this old ant could detect in my tone that I was not asking a question?'

'Yes, Dear Leader.'

'Gredo, I am making you responsible for the construction of the walls for which you will need 350,000,000 large grains of clay. You will be assisted by three other Elders. I have assigned you 4000 masons and ten million workers for the task. The innermost wall is to be 60 antbodies wide and 120 antbodies high. The outer wall is to be 40 antbodies wide and 100 antbodies high. To strengthen the walls your workers are to mix grains of clay with plant hair and fungus that Zekiel will provide, as well as their own vomit. You have twenty days to fulfil this task. You, Elder Gredo, are to be known from this moment onward as Successor to The Dear Leader. You may go.'

'Oh, my Dear Leader, I am honoured that you ——'

'I said, you may go.'

'May I say that I shall serve my Dear Leader by offering up ——'

'Gredo?'

'Yes, Dear Leader?'

'Get out.'

'Yes, Dear Leader.'

He turned to Zekiel. 'You are responsible for the excavation of the moat. The digging will provide Successor Gredo with clay needed to make bricks. The moat will prevent the enemy from digging further tunnels. It will slow the enemy's attack and make them easy targets for my defenders. You have been assigned one million workers. You have twenty days to complete this task. You may go.'

Zekiel did not move.

AyJay Heartland lifted his heavy, lucid eyes and stared unblinkingly at Zekiel.

The old ant chose his words carefully. 'While it is not ant activity that has caused the changes in our empire, you need to know that the level of water in the chambers beneath these rooms you and I are presently in is rising.'

'You said that I need to know.'

'Yes.'

'Yes, who?'

'Yes, Dear Leader.'

'Why do I need to know? You may answer.'

'The defence of our empire is dependent on you remaining secure and enjoying good health.'

'I see. And you are genuinely concerned about the water level.'

'Yes, Dear Leader.'

'Water that can be used to fill the moat,' AyJay Heartland said, 'when you have completed its construction. The water is, therefore, no great concern.'

'There is more I need to tell you, Dear Leader.'

'Speak.'

'I feel it my duty to inform you that the walls Successor Gredo is responsible for will be built on soft sediments that ——'

'That are easily eroded? Is that what you wanted to say to me? Do you think I am not concerned about the rising water level?' He leaned forward, as was his way when emphasising a point, his effusion of pheromones from every part of his exoskeleton causing Zekiel to take one step backwards. 'Perhaps you should dwell on what it is that you do *not* know. The AntLanders are looking to us for leadership. What must one do to be a successful leader? Apart from building walls and a moat, apart from having every physical aspect of our empire ready for an attack, what must we *be*?

'Have you, perhaps, never given any thought to such a question? Then I shall tell you what you have never contemplated: we must *appear* to our subjects as confident and decisive leaders. To be successful, to survive what we are about to endure, we cannot communicate negative pheromonic bulletins to our AntLanders. We must radiate trust. Perception is all. You may go.'

'May I ask about the health of our Queen, Dear Leader?'

'You may not.'

Zekiel made for the exit, walking backwards as he had been instructed by Gredo.

'Stop, Zekiel. Were you acquainted with the ant who made those false claims?'

'No, Dear Leader.'

'Then why did you choose him for your Intercaste Panel?'

'I did not choose him, Dear Leader. The members of his caste chose him.'

'Did he not reveal to you his alarmist views while you were conducting your research?'

'No, Dear Leader.'

AyJay Heartland looked him up and down once, twice, three times. 'I see.'

Silence.

'May I go, Dear Leader?'

'You enquire about the Queen. Her Majesty is giving birth every day to countless Imperial Runners. And others. The birthrate is climbing at an unprecedented level. She is doing her duty for the benefit of AntLand. Go, Zekiel.'

Zekiel made to leave the room.

'Stop. The day The Council met to punish Adam Ant for leaving the empire without permission, something odd occurred. Do you know what I am referring to?'

'No, Dear Leader.'

'The Queen arrived at The Council Chamber the moment Successor Gredo was about to sentence Elder Adam. She was accompanied by a worker, an ordinary worker. One respected but, nonetheless, a worker of no high rank. That lowly worker was you, Zekiel. How was it that you were with the Queen?'

'She had summoned me to escort her.'

'Do you not find that remarkable?'

Zekiel feared responding.

'I am awaiting your response.'

'I do not know why she summoned me, Dear Leader. Perhaps it was only because she wanted information about the journey Adam Ant and I had undertaken. She asked me a question about The Royal Forest not long after I arrived, but before I could answer she decided to go to The Council Chamber. I happened to be with her. She instructed me to accompany her.'

'She should have called for an Imperial Runner or, indeed,

many Imperial Runners. But you? An old ant? Were she to have encountered a threat to her life outside The Royal Chamber, would you, could you have defended her? Saved her?'

'I would give my life for her.'

'Oh, of that I have no doubt, but that is not what I asked.'

'That would depend on the nature of the threat.'

'Ah, what a clever ant you are. You may go, Zekiel.'

Zekiel retreated to the door.

'Wait. What were you thinking when that traitorous ant was about to be executed?'

'I do not recall.'

AyJay Heartland's eyes hardened. 'No, of course not. And of course I was asking the wrong question. My question should have been, what were you feeling?'

'You felt my pheromones.'

'I asked you a question.'

'I was filled with horror.'

'He was a despicable ant. You approved of what he had done?'

'I was filled with horror that I had spent so much time with him and not realised what he was.'

'I see. You may go.'

Zekiel moved towards the exit.

'One more thing.' Zekiel stopped. 'Do you not find it peculiar that prior to rescinding her decision to send Adam Ant to survey the plains, the only appointment the Queen herself made to accompany him was you? After all, who knows what dangers our Former Elder might have encountered?'

'I do not know the workings of our Queen's mind, Dear Leader.'

'Yes. Yes. Of course. Another clever response.'

'And if l may add?'

'You may.'

'There were 100 JourneyAnts present as part of the expedition, Dear Leader. They would have defended the Former Elder against any danger.'

'They would have indeed. They, however, were not chosen by the Queen. Only you were. You are dismissed.'

Zekiel turned towards the door.

'One hundred ants who perished, old ant, while you and Adam Ant survived.'

AyJay Heartland summoned The Imperial Runner he had questioned previously and asked him for a direct, full and truthful response to a question: what, he asked the soldier, did he think of Zekiel the Wise?

'Dear Leader, Zekiel is the most scrupulous, reliable, righteous and trustworthy ant l know.'

'What is the attitude of your fellow Runners?'

'We are of one mind, Dear Leader. Zekiel the Wise is beyond reproach.'

Zekiel was certain that this mad one was leading AntLand to complete destruction. What to do? Oh dear AntGod, what to do?

A revolution was needed. AyJay Heartland had to be deposed. Zekiel had to find a way to make contact with Adam Ant. But how?

With millions of ants coming and going daily from most parts of the empire to the construction site, Zekiel wondered whether he might be able to have his pheromonic thoughts co-expressed from one ant to the next until his master, regardless of where he was being detained, would eventually receive Zekiel's desperate plea for assistance. The trail of transmitted pheromones would, however, be traced back to Zekiel. If he were identified as their source, he knew what the consequences would be – for him, for Adam and the empire.

Zekiel wracked his mind for the rest of that day and all through the night. It was not long after dawn that he thought of a possible solution. He knew the chances of it succeeding were not good ... and yet?

What if, he thought, he released individual pheromonic words and phrases to his worker ants that made no sense? What if he directed these ants to various locations in the metropolis after each day's work had been completed for the purpose of performing other tasks, during which they would, as a matter of course, release these nonsensical signals that would then be detected by Adam? If there were key words or phrases known only to Adam and himself, would Adam realise that a coded message was being sent to him? Would Adam understand that the incoherent, disordered chemosensory proteins had been expressed initially from Zekiel? And that a cryptic method of communication was being employed? That a vital, anguished, distraught message had been embedded amongst disassociated words and phrases and half sentences that he would then have to find a way to combine into an intelligible thought?

Zekiel had no choice. An attempt had to be made. He acted immediately. Hidden within the incomprehensible spillage emanating from his chemical releases Zekiel included, therefore, references to *low-lying clouds* and *snails in hollow logs,* to individual words such as *affront* and *wondrous* and an instruction that one should *lick my mandible.*

Initially Adam thought the baffling chemical expressions were the result of the ants being overworked. It was when multiple ants referred to *the authority of conviction* that he suspected, then felt, Zekiel's presence and was in no doubt at all that it was the thoughts of the wise old ant when several of the worker ants expressed the imperative that *one should not speak in riddles.*

'How well you merit the title the Queen has bestowed upon you, Zekiel, The Royal Sage.'

The Imperial Runners standing guard outside Adam's cell struck the wall with their mandibles. 'Silence!'

It was, Adam thought, a matter of urgency that Zekiel learn he had found a way to decode the messages concealed amongst the discharges of worker ants. Adam understood, as did Zekiel, that a hasty escape was imperative. Embedding the phrases *the certainty in specifics* and *the grasp of intricacies* in his own response, Adam communicated his agreement to the immediate overthrow of AyJay Heartland ... as well as his despair at ever being able to escape from the cell in which he was being held.

It took Zekiel a day and a night to recognise, interpret and then reply to Adam's transmission.

'AntLand cannot afford to have you in despair, Master. You must remain hopeful.'

'My cell is guarded day and night by an Imperial Runner. How am I to escape?'

'It is the nature of all things, Master.'

'No philosophising! Escape! A way must be found!'

'It will be found,' Zekiel communicated in response. 'AntGod sees. AntGod hears.'

'AntGod has deserted us.'

'No, Master. I know this not to be true. How I know, I cannot say. AntGod never meant for us to understand all. Grief is inevitable, as are blessings. Sorrow is the ant's chosen covenant; felicity is AntGod's pledge to us.'

'And were I to escape, who is there to support our revolt? Only the Queen and Nano. But how can we tell her of the necessity to revolt, when we do not where she's been hidden?'

And so Zekiel finally informed Adam of Nano's fate.

'And you tell me AntGod sees? And AntGod hears?'

'Yes, Master, AntGod sees, AntGod hears. We are not alone.'

Teams of Zekiel's labourers had formed a huge circle around the perimeter of The Imperial Gate and, using their mandibles, were working on the excavation for the moat. Individuals carried enormous grains of sand, some ten times their weight, to those laying the foundations for the two walls. Gredo's workers shaped the grains with their own mandibles then lay them in rows, using regurgitated water and vomit as mortar. A smaller team carried away those who died from the heat.

Halfway through the first day of work, one more billboard was erected, counting down the thirty days remaining until the anniversary of the founding of AntLand. Despite the rising death toll, each evening the ants would proudly stand back from their work to see the progress made, before wearily trudging into the metropolis where they received their reduced rations.

Zekiel kept Adam informed of the progress of their work.

Chapter 17

Heat, Hail, Wind

Early one morning, just before the rising of the sun, all activity on the walls and the moat suddenly ceased. Every ant felt a shudder in the earth, a rumbling echo from within the tower. The thunderous sound grew louder with every passing moment, and strange it was, too, that the louder it became the more unmistakable was a peculiar rhythm, a beat accompanied by the chanting of a large number of voices. All eyes turned to the entrance of The Royal Tower and the tower's ventilation shafts that had been thrown open. Millions of ants, faces masked to protect them against the drifting, menacing mass of vapour, waited with bated breath for what was about to reveal itself.

Zekiel climbed to the highest point of the innermost wall to watch AyJay Heartland leading columns of soldier-ants, each one stamping his six feet on the ground as he marched, each combatant making a terrible sound by loudly opening and closing unusually huge mandibles and shouting, in unison, their battle-cry, 'Shock and awe! Shock and awe!'

The workers stood, antennae rigid in astonishment, as an incalculable number of Imperial Runners poured out of the tower and those shafts to reveal all: a dense network of interconnected tunnels, larders, storage rooms and chambers in which Zekiel could clearly see eggs, pupae and vaults of larvae, and fungi gardens, too, thousands of antbody lengths long and hundreds high.

With measured and regular steps the Imperial Runners progressed through the tower's entry and the ventilation shafts, down the steep banks of the moat and past AyJay Heartland, who'd climbed a rock and stood stiffly to attention at a reviewing-point, one antenna saluting his military. The march-past began at dawn. Halfway through the day the last of the soldiers emerged carrying a banner on which had been written the words: *We raise our voices in unison to salute The Dear leader. Long live our Dear Leader. Dying In Defence of The Dear Leader Will Ennoble Us.*

Upon their return to The Royal Tower, the main entry and shafts were again closed.

Military manoeuvres henceforth became a feature of life at AntLand. The preparation for action inspired and comforted the workers. They would, with permission, cease working to watch as the soldiers conducted duels out in the open, their multiplex ball and socket joints swivelling as they scrutinised each other's tactics, whirling one another as they goaded and dared their opponent with pheromonic provocations or, standing upright, attempt to grab their challenger's antennae, mandible or one of their joints; after which these soldiers would rest to sharpen their mandibles or fill their stomachs with formic acid or, balanced on their hind legs, aim blasts of corrosive acid at targets. On one memorable occasion, the workers watched awestruck as the soldiers practised their aim by falling into compact divisions and, with extraordinary rapidity, precision and synchronisation, placed their abdomens under their thoraxes and aimed explosive discharges of acid that immobilised a bird while it was in flight.

And each day, as the Queen gave birth to more soldiers, their numbers swelled and their preparations for battle became more impressive. Even Zekiel, watching the rise of the tower, the meticulous military preparations and the final configuration of the moat and the walls taking shape, could not help but be impressed. As misguided and futile and arrogant as he thought the defensive preparations and the construction of The Royal Tower to be, he was proud of his fellow AntLanders. They were tireless and conscientious, but they were also naïve, misguided and gullible.

Every morning, not long after work had begun and the sun had risen, he looked up at the pale, cloudless sky and the brooding horizon. He considered the limitless tattered limbs of trees lying on the ground and wondered how it was that no-one could see what he saw: the earth bristled in the heat, the odour and terrible glare; the air was becoming thinner and, with each passing week, the sky itself was being bled dry. In the metropolis itself, clouds of mist, ashen and ghostly, strayed along passages and thoroughfares, drifting out of The Imperial Gate to merge with some dense palpitating notion of death, a spectacular throbbing *thing* that clung to the tower in some shocking embrace aglow with nightmarish foreboding. His foragers and hunters – those left to him and not conscripted by AyJay Heartland for the construction of chambers for the soldiers the Queen was producing – returned with fewer seeds and prey. AyJay refused to supplement the labourers' rations from their vast number of vaults, rooms and chambers so that, should the worst occur, they would be able to withstand a long siege. What they ate was what Zekiel's hunters and gatherers collected; while his ants labouring on the tower suffered as they went back and forth, endlessly carrying grains of clay to Gredo's workers. Face masks clogged, and in the middle of each day, when the blurred haze was at its heaviest, many ants fell sick with stiff antennae joints, giddiness, violent vomiting and shortness of breath. Each day more and more of them succumbed and, within a few days, died.

Zekiel regularly communicated with Adam, alerting him to the progress made in the construction of The Royal Tower, the oppressive conditions under which his former workers laboured and, most importantly, the tight control AyJay Heartland's Runners exercised over his movements.

Adam's ciphered response conveyed his despondency. 'If you don't find a way to Her Majesty, we face destruction.'

'Gratitude is a key element of our concordat with AntGod, Master.'

'Gratitude that He has deserted us?'

'That He has given us the means of restoration so that we be improved beyond measure.'

'Are you both foolish and wise, Zekiel?'

Meanwhile, guided tours of the construction site continued for the ants who lived permanently in the city and had never seen the light of day. Those who maintained the seed vaults and the fungi gardens, were nursemaids to the young and took care of the Queen's hygiene needs saw for themselves the mighty efforts of their fellow AntLanders. They gasped to see the perfect symmetry of the concentric walls and their tremendous thickness; they marvelled at the depth of the moat; they shook their antennae in wonder at the sight of millions of workers going about their tireless work in harmony, the diggers following their own pheromone trails while the brick builders followed theirs, no one ant disturbing the task of another. The pride they felt was communicated to these labourers, who responded with even greater efforts, chanting 'Big-ger! Bet-ter! Best!' and 'Long live our Dear Leader!' as they worked.

Fifteen days before the anniversary celebrations, the heaviest hailstorm anyone could recall struck AntLand, forcing the workers into the city. It lasted until the middle of the day, when the sky cleared and the intense heat returned. That night, as the ants tried to sleep, wild winds battered the walls and the tower. The ants shuddered at the terrific noise of the storm. It whistled and groaned for hour upon hour, millions of ants huddling in fear when they felt the tower itself shift on its own foundations. The winds even flew through the passageways and thoroughfares, a shrill whirlwind assaulting their city like some revengeful monster. They feared they would venture out when the winds had died down to be greeted by the terrible sight of the tower in ruins, its collapse bringing down sections of the walls and filling the moat with debris. One ant foolishly wondered out aloud if AntGod was punishing AntLand because, all those months ago, the

Queen had left The Royal Chamber to address her subjects, something unprecedented in the life of the empire.

The early morning revealed their triumph. The tower stood, majestic and intact. The walls were exactly as they had left them, imposing and stately. AyJay emerged to inspect the site. He gave a stirring speech, congratulating the workers on the quality of their labour. He said that such unparalleled and severe changes in the weather were so unnatural that they could only have been created by the enemy. AntLand, however, had withstood all that the barbarian could throw at them. If the empire could hold firm against alien-inspired hailstorms and hurricanes, then its future was secure. He led the workers in chanting the empire's refrain then, when that was done, demanded their attention.

He said: 'In this time of need, when AntLand faces the greatest threat it has ever known, internal criticism cannot be allowed to undermine all that we have thus far achieved. I demand that the ant who questioned whether AntGod was punishing the empire because of the appearance of the Queen outside her chamber step forward.'

The following day, this ant appeared before a mysterious committee of ants established by AyJay Heartland, known as The Imperial Protectors. The ant was not seen again.

Ten days before the anniversary, when the oppressive sun stood still and detached, Zekiel felt a gently-moving breeze. He climbed out of the moat, his shadow dark and sinister in the white-hot day, and searched the air with his antennae. Everywhere he looked workers had stopped to savour the relief; but there was something that disturbed Zekiel. The day glowed. A terrible timelessness had settled on the valley and, in the unrelieved fierce light, he saw a tiny cloud of dust rise in a circular motion many antbodies away from the building site. Plumes of fine sand hung in the air then settled on the ground. Irregular, vacillating and vague waves of dust rose then fell, rose again, then fell, fluctuating in odd movements. And then the world became still. The ants, disappointed that the breeze had died, returned to work. Zekiel sought shelter inside the metropolis then climbed alone to the highest point of Gredo's walls, stood on his rear legs and scanned the air.

There was a troubling silence, a deadened noise, an aching, sharp prickling sensation he could not comprehend. Fine grains of sand flitted about his face. Each grain was warm. He looked through the colourless haze towards the horizon. He saw an exhausted landscape that was now stirring, saw some indefinable body drifting across the valley. Something was awakening, not the feet of soldiers but something else, some monster, unseen and mysterious, was that very moment rising out of the red, dusty earth. Dead leaves rustled. The dried out remains of a lizard rolled until its progress was caught by a sun-bleached rock. White bones of branches shifted. Dry branches as far as the eye could see stirred to life. As the workers laboured, they watched in silence as strangely-coloured clouds at one moment rose, swelled, groaned and heaved against each other, at the next hung motionless in a glowering lull.

The AntLanders resumed digging. They carried soil from the moat to the wall. They created and laid bricks. But all twenty-one million ants felt their exoskeletons tighten and their antennae become rigid. Some instinctive understanding urged them to take refuge in the metropolis. One by one they stopped working and stared in wonder as the malignant shadow of some uneasy presence changed the colour of the sun. Elder Gredo ordered them back to work. Many looked towards Zekiel for direction. Gredo once more issued his order, which most ants ignored. Outraged that he had not been obeyed, the Elder pushed past several workers, knocking them to the ground.

Gredo marched into the city, the ground shuddering when he returned with several hundred soldiers, the likes of which no AntLander had ever seen. The soldiers were certainly of their species, but these ants were twice as big as any ant the Queen had ever given birth to, with tough, protective, chitin-plated armour, powerful sinewy legs, massive, helmeted spear like heads, two spines angled to their rear for protection, barbs fortifying their neck and sharp-toothed, blood-red, scythe-shaped mandibles so large it was a wonder these soldiers could stand erect. Gredo ordered them to fall into line between the moat and the outermost wall. Two of his soldiers seized an ant and, with their antennae exuding repulsive, pervasive pheromones, severed his head in one swift movement. Millions of ants cried out in horror. Zekiel made to move towards the Elder, but his path was immediately blocked by two soldiers who turned to face him, their jaws open wide and their mandibles held high. He ordered them to stand aside. They ignored him. Nothing like this had ever happened in the life of the empire.

Gredo then delivered their Dear Leader's decree. 'Henceforth, if discipline is not imposed by the individual upon himself, it will be imposed upon him by the empire. The survival of AntLand is paramount.

'Henceforth, work on the moat and the walls will be closely monitored by Her Majesty's elite force, The Red Mandibles.'

Red Mandibles? AntLand had an elite force?

'Henceforth,' said Elder Gredo, 'work on the moat and the walls is to commence two hours before dawn and cease two hours after sunset. Resume your labour. Immediately.'

Zekiel, incredulous, stared in amazement at these huge, fearsome soldiers. Who but the Queen could have produced these menacing warriors? But why? Was it possible she had done so on condition that Adam Ant's life was spared? Or simply to do what she could to prepare AntLand for the coming war?

All the ants returned to work, stunned that their empire would resort to such barbarity, their eyes and antennae focused at one moment on the threatening presence of the Red Mandibles, at the other on the deepening orange hue of the sun, the whistling wind agitating the dry ground and the landscape of stirring dead weeds, bushes and trees.

Zekiel approached Gredo. 'I am going to order my workers to cease work. I am going to order my workers to immediately retreat into the city.'

'I have my orders,' said Gredo. 'Action will be taken if you disobey!'

But Zekiel did not have to order his labourers into the city. They all stood, breathless and amazed, as day began to turn into night. The sun had become a blood red ball, burning lucent, hanging surly in an impenetrable sky. Panic gripped the workers. Masks were tightly secured. They watched helplessly as an enormous, seething black-yellow cloud rolled towards them, as if the gates of The Great Darkness beyond the cliffs had been thrown open. Dry, furious, windblown blasts of hot dust merged, swirling with the poisonous odour to converge in a matter of moments on the entire worksite, the gales assaulting the ants with terrific force, taking hold of some of the workers scurrying down The Royal Tower, lifting them bodily into the sky then dropping them from some unseen height on those blindly scrambling over each other in a frenzied attempt to pass through The Imperial Gate. The cloud was so hot and fell upon them with such howling speed that many wondered if the world had been set alight. Fine particles of hot, whirling dust rained upon them, penetrating their eyes, coating their antennae, finding their way into their joints and even down their throats, drying up the moisture in their lungs. The valley was whipped by shifting, nauseous, billowing shrouds that reduced visibility to a few antbodies. Zekiel threw himself into the dry moat, dug a small opening in its side into which he took refuge and covered the opening just before the empire was plunged into an oppressive darkness.

Thousands of ants were trampled to death, while at least as many died of suffocation or were burnt alive by the scalding caustic wind. It continued for hour upon hour, and Zekiel, unable to see his own claw in front of his eyes, could do little but shut his senses to the distraught cries of the wounded and dying and the prayers to AntGod that went unanswered.

Zekiel stayed in his shelter all night, thinking. The dust storm had come from the direction of The Sacred Circle. What had so severely affected AntLand had just as severely affected the enemy, the only difference being that the enemy had no reserve supplies of food. An invasion, therefore, was imminent. Adam needed to be told.

Exhausted and in despair, Zekiel placed his head on the ground and fell within moments to sleep.

A short time later, he abruptly awoke, wide-eyed and clear-headed. Of course! he cried out loud. How could he not have realised. Fool! Fool, that you are! Zekiel the Fool, not Zekiel the Wise. He recalled climbing the innermost moat wall and watching AyJay Heartland leading his soldier-ants out of the uncompleted Royal Tower, each one crying out, 'Shock and awe! Shock and awe!' He recollected looking down into ventilation openings and doors where he saw linked tunnels, larders overflowing with food, storage rooms and chambers in which he spied eggs and pupae, and enormous fungi gardens which had been positioned near arched rooms full of larvae. And, Zekiel knew, somewhere inside that vast structure, close to her pupae and eggs, was the imprisoned Queen.

And so did Adam who, in the panic, minutes after the red-hot storm had howled through the thoroughfare of The Royal Tower and knocked senseless to the ground the Red Mandible standing guard outside his chamber, ran out of his cell, rushed from chamber to path, path to thoroughfare, thoroughtfare to larders and tunnels and secret passages, looking for the Queen.

Chapter 18

Fire

When Zekiel emerged in the morning, all was quiet and still. It was a grim, hazy dawn. A fierce sun beat down upon an exhausted earth. Dust blanketed the scarred ground that bore little resemblance to the world he had known. With every step he took, fine powder rose whirling in tiny clouds, drifting dryly in the ashen incandescent sky. He wandered alone amongst the jumbled, whitened corpses of AntLanders. Many had been burnt alive, their bodies shrivelled into unsightly contortions. Others had dashed to their death leaping from the tower. Some showed no sign of injury. These, Zekiel thought, had either died from inhaling smoke or suffocated in the mad scramble to get into the metropolis. This was clearly evident from the enormous pile of bodies outside The Imperial Gate. He estimated that some 10,000 ants had perished.

He walked through the ominous glow of this, his dreadful world, his every pore choking with dust, to see what had remained of those forests in which his hunters searched for prey. These were now mostly cratered, parched and crusted. As far as he could see the vegetation was predominantly that of withered and shrivelled dead grass, weeds and shrubs. Little had survived. Dead leaves and branches, corpses and rocks had been blown into disorderly mounds. Any moisture that remained in the soil after the long, eleven months of relentless heat had been baked dry by the fiery air. Now there was the putrid smell of slow and painful death. In the distance, aphids and caterpillars searched vainly for something to eat, the movement of the creatures setting the dust in motion. Amidst the rolling, curling clouds were honeypot ants, which had, it seemed to Zekiel, lost their minds, fleeing in panic from the safety of their chambers deep underground and out onto the surface. He watched, perplexed, as they devoured the honeydew supply of one another's distended gaster. Those that had survived wandered confused in the wasteland.

There was no choice. If the citizens of AntLand were to avoid starving to death, they had to eat from the supplies of food AyJay Heartland had intended keeping in reserve should the aliens lay siege to the metropolis.

A hot breeze tightened Zekiel's exoskeleton. He watched with antennae made erect, as it stirred the dead leaves and branches. A white-hot presence blurred The Sacred Circle. The clifftops became distorted as the breeze grew in intensity and shifted direction, tiny hot embers flitting about his face. Sensing some new danger, he looked with cold detachment over the twisted corpses, through the exhausted landscape to a hollow, quivering glimmer. The valley began to writhe, contort and buckle. It appeared to lift itself then fall, shimmering in some strange buffeting of sky and earth and wind. He watched the nightmare unfold as his world was hauled up then tossed about in a series of fiery explosions.

A huge seething wall of fire, some sixty antbodies high, was racing towards AntLand. He saw the dry grasslands, the dead branches and the skeletons of trees explode as the flames, transformed into a beastly red-hot tempest, tumbling down then up out of gullies, incinerating everything in its path. Smoke and fire became one, as the quivering roaring monster swept heaving across the valley.

Zekiel rushed to The Imperial Gate, threw aside body after body and crawled into the city. He rose to his feet and ran, noting – what a strange thing to consider at such a moment, he thought! – the thick layer of dust that had penetrated every crevice, every vault, every room. In several chambers terrified livestock huddled in fear, making strange helpless sounds. He gathered as many ants as he could, his pheromones alerting them of the new threat. Through these ants he issued orders. His former foragers and hunters were to rush to the lowest chambers, fill their mouths with water and douse the moat, walls and tower. Ten were selected to enter the private chambers off The War Rooms and alert AyJay Heartland of the grave threat to the metropolis. Livestock handlers were to immediately round up the wandering caterpillars and aphids and return them to their pens, farmers to conscript as many workers as they could to soak the passageways leading to their storage of food and to clear the area surrounding AntLand of all dry matter.

To gain a clearer view of the approaching fire and the fire-fighting efforts of the AntLanders, Zekiel ran outside and mounted the outside wall of the tower. He was almost swept off the structure by extreme winds that drove the firewall over the dry grasslands. Fiery walls now reached a height of eighty antbodies. As he watched, they seemed to die away only to return from a different direction. He descended the tower and instructed his farmers to marshal foragers and hunters to different parts of the moat and walls and tower. Dense smoke, extreme heat, dust clouds and spot fires hindered the efforts of all. To make matters worse, the winds kept changing direction, sweeping burning branches dangerously close to The Imperial Gate.

And then the miracle happened. It had to have been AntGod Himself intervening. Moments after the arrival of AyJay Heartland, the moat began, seemingly of its own accord, to fill up with water. It was as if some spring had burst open beneath the moat. The water, ice-cold and pure, seeped into the lower sections of the ditch, supplying those who doused the tower, the entry into the metropolis and the walls with all the water they needed, creating also a barrier that the fire could not cross. Foragers, hunters, livestock handlers, farmers, workers, Imperial Runners and Red Mandibles joined forces. They filled their mouths with water from the moat and ran back and forth until all the fires threatening the empire had been either beaten back or completely extinguished. And if any ant needed confirmation that it was AntGod Himself Who had intervened, the flow of water ceased once the moat was filled to its capacity.

The threat had passed. The flames had moved on well beyond AntLand, blackening the surrounding landscape. Thousands of brave firefighters had lost their lives, but at least the metropolis had been saved. A confusion of haze and smoke and heat blanketed the charred earth, shifting and rising over gnarled and blackened limbless stumps of trees.

Zekiel climbed down from the tower to assist in carrying the dead to the gravesite, where a funeral ceremony would be held at an appropriate time. He paused at the entry to the tower which, in the general confusion, had been left unguarded.

Zekiel's mind was racing. Had an opportunity presented itself? Much of the empire's livestock had inexplicably fled the safety of their chambers during the fire. Hundreds of worker ants had perished in the panic to get into the metropolis. He looked again at the aphids and caterpillars, some wandering aimlessly in shock while others were nestling together in fear. All appeared exposed, vulnerable. He watched as hunters and gatherers, foragers, livestock-handlers and farmers joined forces with The Imperial Runners and The Red Mandibles, all under AyJay Heartland's direction, to restore order to the empire. Yes, perhaps, just perhaps, in all this confusion and distraction ...

He looked this way and that to ensure that no Imperial Runner or Red Mandible was present and entered The Tower.

Minutes later, Zekiel's antennae stood involuntarily erect. He felt strange palpitations in his entire body, a loosening of his limbs as if he were breaking apart. He frantically ran his antennae over the ground, the walls and the ceiling to confirm what he knew to be there. There was no doubt. He recognised the scent. It was that of an alien! Somewhere in the tower the Queen had been hidden. Was Zekiel too late to save her? Which way to turn in that vast structure? Which passageway to take? The obvious answer eluded him for a moment or two, and then he knew: follow the alien's scent.

He heard a rumble of footsteps and threw himself into

a crevice in the wall as hundreds of Red Mandibles ran past him, oblivious of his presence. But their feet had broken the trail of the alien! And now? What now? Before he could decide on his next course of action he felt himself seized by one of his front legs, pulled out of the crevice and dragged up a steep thoroughfare. He fought to break free from his abductor: a Red Mandible?

Or was it? This ant was neither tall nor muscular, and yet he had the mandibles, insignia and uniform of one who belonged to that elite squad.

'The Queen!' Zekiel cried. 'She is in danger. An alien ——'

'Come!'

'No, you do not understand.'

'No, *you* do not understand. Come! Quickly!'

'Listen to me. An alien is in the tower.'

'I know.'

'You know? You know? Who are you? *What* are you?'

'Follow me!'

The ant released Zekiel from his hold and ran up a maze of passages, some with the ceiling constructed so low, for reasons of security, that they had to press down hard on the ground to crawl through to the other side. Zekiel followed as the ant climbed up and through interconnecting rooms, into and along tunnels concealed beneath pens containing aphids and through secret doors behind enormous chambers of seeds. They fought through mountains of fungi at the end of which were tiny openings in the ground leading to a bewildering network of narrow, steep tunnels which they crawled down, their stomachs scraping the ground and their antennae folded back. The ant leading Zekiel stopped at a humble chamber.

From one of the ventilation openings they heard millions of voices cry in unison. The funeral ceremony had probably begun, thought Zekiel.

The ant stepped out of his uniform, removed the insignia and detached the huge mandibles which, it was immediately clear to Zekiel, had once belonged to the soldier who had been guarding him, and removed his helmet. It was Adam.

He opened the door to the chamber. Adam entered, then touched the ground with the top of his head in obeisance. There was the Queen. To her right stood the yellow alien.

Chapter 19

The Enemy Approaches

'Arise, Adam. No ceremony, Zekiel. Approach.'

Adam took up position to the left of the Queen while Zekiel, bewildered by the sudden turn of events, remained standing at the threshold, his mouth open, his antennae bristling, all his eyes darting confusedly here and there.

'Zekiel, if you wish to contribute to the saving of AntLand we suggest you move. Come, stand before us. Here. We have much to discuss and very little time.'

'Your Majesty, this alien was the one who left pheromones at the campsite and who ——'

'Left you with a request,' said the alien.

'He left us with a demand! And, Your Majesty, a threat!'

'He has come alone, Zekiel. During the chaos that you, we are grateful to see, survived.'

Zekiel approached the alien. He ran his antennae over the alien's head, thorax and abdomen.

'Are you satisfied now that I come in goodwill?' the yellow ant said. 'I have had many opportunities to play the assassin, if it had been my aim to kill the Princess or your

Queen, Zekiel. I am,' he said, 'your only hope. The request I delivered was my own. The demand and the threat were given on behalf of others. It is those *others* whom you should fear, not me.'

'If what you say is true, what do you expect to achieve?' Zekiel said to the yellow ant. He turned to Adam and the Queen. 'The moment this ambassador is seen ... Wait. How did you enter The Royal Tower? How is it that you were not seen?'

'The dust storm and the fire provided cover.'

'During both of which the ambassador could have died, Zekiel,' said the Queen.

'And how,' Zekiel said to Adam, 'did you find the Queen?'

'There was,' said Adam, 'one pheromonic trail with a scent made unique simply because it had been traversed many, many times. The amount of pheromones deposited created a trail that was deep and wide and quite overpowering in chemicals that communicated awe and respect and fear. The ambassador and I came upon it separately. We both guessed correctly that wherever it led was a place of great importance. And so it led to Her Majesty.'

'But the moment you are seen,' Zekiel said to the yellow ant, 'you will be killed. Why have you come here alone? You are alone, I presume?'

'I am.'

'Enough. We have little time for explanations,' said the Queen. 'Suffice to say that we have been in a position to make certain demands, despite being a prisoner. We refused to produce Red Mandibles unless Adam's life was spared and we were given assurances that you, Zekiel, would be allotted to Adam as a bodyguard if and when the aliens attacked our metropolis.'

'Bodyguard?' said Adam.

'Yes, Adam Ant. In time you will learn why.'

'But, Your Majesty, if we're attacked I must fight alongside — —'

'Silence, Adam. We must make haste.'

'And what of the Princess? Who will guard her?'

'Adam Ant! Plans have been made! Enough talking. Our esteemed Elder Ambassador here has risked his life in taking this final opportunity to avert war. Speak, Elder Ambassador.'

The alien bowed to the Queen. 'The army ants have wrested control of The Coalition of the Willing from the Argentine ants. They have done so through their sheer number, their brutal methods and with the support of the red ants and the fire ants. There are over forty million soldiers assembling while we speak. They make ready to attack. You are vulnerable to an immediate assault because – and you know this – of their desperation. They have nothing to lose. It is true: they *are* dying of starvation. Every day, countless ants are found dead from lack of food. The army ants rule by terror. My last and perhaps only hope is that those whom they rule would accept another species of ant as leader if they were not facing a slow death. What I mean is this: they would join with whoever can guarantee their survival. This coming war is about food. Nothing more.'

'What must we do, Ambassador?' said the Queen.

'There is no time for negotiations, no time for words. This is the reason I risked my life in coming here. You must act immediately. You must leave this chamber, send representatives to The Sacred Circle of Cliffs to inform those preparing to invade that they will be given food, then marshal your workers and take whatever you can to them before nightfall. Those ants must see that food is on the way. That is the only way you will undermine the power of the warmongers, and, believe me – you must believe me – there are many of those.'

Adam looked towards Zekiel. They had, they knew, a warmonger of their own.

'The attempt must be made,' said the Queen, 'otherwise we might all perish. In this moment of grieving we must seize our opportunity. We shall speak to our subjects. We shall interrupt the funeral and we shall inform AntLanders that we shall assume control. Our hope is that AyJay Heartland will not dare contradict us before our subjects, although we cannot assume that he will not attempt to do so.' The Queen turned to the alien. 'Ambassador, should we succeed, should our subjects understand the dire situation we are in and agree to send food to your allies, you will be given safe passage to your ants. You will be accompanied by Zekiel. Should we fail, however, you will undoubtedly be apprehended and immediately executed. We thank you for your bravery. Zekiel the Wise, escort us to the cemetery.' She paused. 'We have not set foot on the outside world for almost 400 months. Our subjects will be horrified. It will, we trust, be a sign to them of the gravity of our situation. We enter a new world. Old traditions, old ways of doing things are soon to go.' She turned to face Adam. 'You will recall what we had said previously, dear Adam, when we asked the Elders to leave us at the last Council meeting. When the time comes, we might well instruct you to do something which goes against your better instincts. You must do as we say without hesitation. You must trust us. Give us your word that you will do as we instruct.'

'Yes, my Queen.'

'So that there is no misunderstanding, we clarify our demand: You will not join the battle. Under no circumstances are you to join the defence of our kingdom.'

He hesitated.

'Swear!'

'I do swear, Your Majesty.'

'Come. We go. Elder Ambassador, the only thing between you and death is our ability to sway our subjects. Remain in this chamber, Adam. It is of the greatest importance that your life is spared.'

Another great cry was heard from the cemetery, and then silence. Adam looked out the ventilation opening. All the ants who had gathered to mourn the dead were staring at The Sacred Circle of Cliffs. Adam saw what they saw and heard what they heard: smoke and bristling embers swirled about the cliff face, transforming the horizon into an indistinct, pale, thrumming presence. Adam was joined by the others, all of whom looked into the vague distance and, listening for a clarification of the swelling sound drumming, humming in the suffocating world, felt a vague stirring, a slight trembling in the air. They stared hard into that world made vague with smoke and dust and the shimmering heat of a hostile sun. A slight breeze opened a narrow vista through which those at the cemetery and those in the tower could see The Sacred

Circle, now without any snow at all. The melted snow, Adam and Zekiel knew, had no doubt poured into the chasm. Some would filter into deep underground chambers ... damaging, perhaps, the foundations of the metropolis.

And then the faces of all at the ventilation shaft were contorted in horror, their entire exoskeletons turned rigid, their antennae tense and hard and extended. A vast shadow was making its way over the edge of the cliff and down into The Eternal Valley. The slope that Adam and Zekiel had climbed almost twelve months previously was now concealed by an army of ants that resembled a vast shifting veil. The enemy was on the move. The battle to save AntLand was about to begin.

'Too late!' cried the alien. 'We are all too late!'

Adam and Zekiel rushed to the doorway of the chamber to see that the way was clear to evacuate the Queen to a safe location. Safe? Where, they both wondered, might that be?

And AyJay Heartland, standing on a knoll from which he had been delivering a stirring eulogy, chose that moment to look towards where he knew the Queen to be. He saw two faces at the ventilation shaft. One of them was yellow. AyJay pointed to the opening and cried, 'Alien!' Thirty million ants turned as one and saw their Queen, held captive, they assumed, by the enemy. Aliens had found their way into the Queen's chamber! How was that possible? Her life was in danger!

AyJay Heartland had his Imperial Runners secure the entry to The Royal Tower to hold back the mourners who were eager to charge en masse into the building to save her. This was, he told them, a rescue mission that only his Red

Mandibles could undertake. Successor Gredo received his instructions. With the eyes of the whole empire upon them, he and 1000 elite soldiers stormed the tower.

The Queen, observing all, turned to the alien. 'There is,' she said, 'nothing we can do. Forgive us. Zekiel, protect Adam. You must preserve his life. Swear.'

'I swear.'

'On your life.'

'On my life.'

'Elder Ambassador, we ask again that you forgive us for what we are about to do. Zekiel! Adam! Apprehend this alien! Do as we say! Pin him to the ground!'

Moments later, Successor Gredo burst into the room.

'Gredo,' said the Queen, 'we welcome your presence. As you can see, your Queen has been saved. We are grateful to AntGod for sending Former Elder Adam and Zekiel the Wise who have rescued me from the clutches of this assassin.'

'Adam Ant, you have escaped from the cell in which ——'

'Gredo! Were these two unable to come to our aid, do you realise that your Queen would have been executed?'

Successor Gredo cried: 'But I am here, Your Majesty! With our Mandibles!'

'Late, Gredo. How, may we ask, did this assassin find a way into The Royal Tower? Why were your Mandibles unable to protect your sovereign? Adam Ant and Zekiel the Wise are heroes. They are to be treated as saviours. We demand that they be given due honour. Do you want your failure to protect us during this time of crisis to be overlooked?'

Successor Gredo had two of his Red Mandibles seize then drag the terrified alien out of The Royal Tower.

Zekiel was given the honour of a Mandibular Procession to the cemetery. The Queen, remaining in the chamber, returned to the ventilation shaft with Adam and two Red Mandibles on either side of them. She waved at her subjects with both her antennae. A mighty roar greeted her appearance. She had been rescued! The Dear Leader had rescued their Queen! He had acted decisively, giving these aliens the first of what would undoubtedly be many defeats! Without any prompting by AyJay Heartland, millions of ants turned towards the cliff face and the enemy and cried, 'Big-ger! Bet-ter! Best! Ant-Land! Ant-Land! Ant-Land! Shock and awe! Shock and awe!' and then, with the encouragement of some Red Mandibles, 'Ay-Jay! Ay-Jay! Ay-Jay!'

Successor Gredo relayed to AyJay Heartland what had transpired in the Queen's chamber. AyJay looked up at The Royal Tower. The Queen had remained at the ventilation opening, watching him, her antennae quivering.

He turned to the gathering. This was not a time to provoke the Queen's displeasure. He well knew what she demanded of him. 'Ants of the Empire, devotees of our Queen, Successor Gredo has informed me that prior to my Red Mandibles storming our Queen's chamber, Former Elder Adam Ant and Zekiel the Wise had apprehended this alien. We are and will always be grateful to these faithful servants. Let us show our appreciation by acclamation.'

AyJay Heartland called for quiet. He had the alien dragged to the knoll. 'Here is the evidence. Now you know why it has been necessary to impose martial law and a state of emergency. What, my fellow AntLanders, should we do with this assassin? It is, let us not forget, these aliens who have come to conquer us. You can see for yourselves; they are on the march. It is not we who chose to conquer them. Who, I ask you, is the aggressor? They or us?'

'They!'

'And it is they who have infiltrated our very metropolis to butcher our Queen. Did we threaten the life of any of their queens?'

'No!'

'And it is they who have made demands that we give them food. Have we made demands on them for food?'

'No!'

'Should we show this assassin mercy?'

'None! None! None!'

AyJay Heartland instructed four Red Mandibles to go down to the empire's cells and return with a butterfly that had been kept alive so that it could be butchered when there was a need for fresh meat. He then turned to two other Mandibles. 'Do your patriotic duty to this assassin.'

The soldiers collaborated, with one holding the writhing alien by his two rear legs, another by his two front legs. They pulled at the extremities with the hooked claws at the end of their feet until the alien's body was taut. A third, who surely had the biggest mandibles in the entire empire, slowly climbed onto the knoll. He stood above the squirming, hysterical alien who was emitting high-pitched squeals. The Queen and Adam stepped away from the shaft in her chamber, while Zekiel closed his eyes so that they would not witness the horror which was about to unfold. The executioner lowered his mandibles then amputated one of the alien's legs. He held it above his head to the mighty clamour of the onlookers. He then proceeded to slice off every leg in turn, each one held aloft like some ghastly trophy. The limbless ant, screaming in pain, was lifted high by the two soldiers, while the executioner turned to the onlookers, opening and closing his mandibles.

'Kill! Kill! Kill!' they cried.

He decapitated the ant.

AyJay turned to the butterfly. 'You have one mission to perform. Should you fail to complete the task I am assigning to you, you will die a most horrible death should we ever catch you. Complete the task, and you will have your freedom. Your answer?'

The butterfly took to the air as soon as the Ambassador's dismembered parts were fastened to its body, his mission being to unload the legs, antennae, thorax and head over the enemy camp.

As soon as the insect had taken to the sky, AyJay Heartland ordered a thousand Red Mandibles to accompany Elder Gredo to The Holy Reliquary, where the consecrated grains of soil upon which the Queen had landed almost 400 months previously had been placed for safekeeping. The sacred casket containing the relics was removed ceremonially from the secret shrine and carried to the surface. Every citizen of AntLand was ordered to assemble in a mighty circle around The Royal Tower and The Imperial Gate and watch, in reverence, as AyJay Heartland walked alone, dressed in his regal gown, holding in his outstretched hands the container that had long preserved those sanctified relics. Once The Dear Leader had completed the procession, he walked with much solemnity to the highest point of the inner wall and held the casket high above his head. Thirty million ants immediately prostrated themselves, their hearts fit to burst, knowing that with AntGod's assistance, victory in the coming war was assured.

Chapter 20

War

Their optimism was short-lived. The morning after the execution, the steep side of the cliff was again completely covered by enemy ants. AntLanders gathered on the completed outer wall and the high points of the unfinished inner wall to watch in silence as this dark flow of death poured into their valley. Some prayed. Others trembled in horror. Adam and Zekiel feared the worst. No boulder, no crevice, no glimpse of dry earth could be seen beneath this menacing presence that took the whole of the morning to descend in rigid military lines towards the base of The Sacred Circle of Cliffs. The slope was finally revealed when the last of the ants had taken his position on the valley floor. There was a collective sigh of relief amongst the AntLanders. The number of enemy soldier-ants was not as numerous as they had feared. Optimism was renewed.

Hours passed. There was no activity as the enemy ants maintained their formation. What, AntLanders wondered, were they waiting for?

Their question was answered late in the afternoon of that same day when the cliff metamorphosed into what resembled a heaving, throbbing forest, as countless green ants swept down its face to join their coalition partners, this avalanche of ants continuing as the sun fell. Pessimism reasserted itself.

In response, the worker ants labouring on the final stages of the inner wall and the uppermost levels of the tower had their number vastly increased. Livestock, bred or captured for their meat, had their death sentence commuted so that they could assist. Aphids, caterpillars and ladybirds, honeypot ants and the ants who had never known physical labour, such as those attending to the personal needs of the Queen, were conscripted. They toiled virtually all night in pitch darkness, regularly glancing towards the cliff, wondering what would greet them when the sun rose. They were allowed a mere two hours' sleep.

When awoken at dawn, they were overjoyed to see, with the rising of the sun, what they thought was the entire cliff face ablaze. Despondency then set in, when they realised it was not an out-of-control bushfire that had overwhelmed the cliff, but an endless discharge of red ants.

For three days in succession ants of many species flowed into the valley, like some bizarre waterfall that kept changing colour. From the windows and ventilator shafts of their respective rooms, the Queen, Adam and Zekiel watched as the enemy assembled, millions of ants waiting patiently and in strict order for the command to begin marching across the valley floor, a tremulous throng of starving aliens. It was on the fourth day, when work on the inner wall and the tower was finally completed, that the pouring of ants down the cliff ceased and their march commenced.

Adam watched their perfectly synchronised advance. These were not ants who had been born savage, he thought, but were, rather, ants that had been driven to acts of desperation because of circumstances beyond their control. Was it not their AntGod-given nature to do what was required to stay alive, for their own sake and that of their own kind?

And so it was that Adam realised what should have been obvious to him and all his fellow AntLanders all along: the enemy, like him, like Zekiel, like AyJay Heartland, like the Queen herself were of the same species. Their God and his was one and the same. They were all – the green, the yellow, the tiny, the huge – of one kind. What did this mean? It meant that the prayers of the AntLanders were futile. It meant that AntGod would not favour AntLand. Oh, if only they had all realised what was so plainly obvious when the request for sustenance had been initially made!

And yet, despite all this, he would stay by his Queen's side and do all he could to defend her. He would even kill, yes, those who had simply been driven into taking extreme measures because they wanted to survive.

After many days and nights of continual marching, the enemy approached close enough for Adam and Zekiel to take note of the huge-mandibled officers of many colours running alongside the uniform flanks of soldiers. For intimidatory effect, they would occasionally break off to gather in groups to whet their trenchant mandibles and, it appeared, make decisions. Adam and Zekiel followed closely the manner in which the enemy ants maintained an impressive, perfect formation, tightly organising themselves into battalions according to species. Leading the march was an infantry of ants big and small, stocky and slender, a coalition of every colour and species: many were armoured with an outer covering of jagged, serrated plates, while others either swivelled in time their abdomen beneath their thorax to display their toxin-filled abdomens or held their filed and honed spear-like antennae as they marched. This compact group led a teeming, swarming mass, which levelled and destroyed almost everything in its swift advance.

Zekiel joined Adam and the Queen in The Royal Chamber.

'Why destroy everything in their path, Zekiel? Why go to all that trouble?'

'Do you not see, Adam,' said the Queen, 'what this tells us? They are making it impossible for any deserting AntLander to escape the metropolis unseen.'

It was clear to them, then, that the enemy was bent not only on the plunder of AntLand but also its destruction.

'They are fearsome, Master.'

'And mightily impressive, Zekiel. I fear it. I fear what is to unfold.'

Zekiel took Adam to one side: 'If they should overpower AntLand, Master, we must save Her Majesty. If the metropolis falls, AntLand's only hope of survival lies in helping her escape.'

'The tunnel?'

'Yes.'

'I shall fight, Master, and probably perish. You, however, are destined to assist the Queen in her escape. You must resist the temptation to engage in the conflict. Remember your pledge, Master.'

The enemy approached with shocking precision as one being, a throbbing, insatiable, writhing beast voraciously consuming every dry leaf, every charred branch in its path. Millions of AntLanders watched horrified as some of the aliens, long-necked and with sharp spikes on their backs, fell roughshod upon the corpses of AntLanders who had only recently died in the duststorm and fire. Other aliens – with heavily-armoured bodies and antennae protected by frontal carinae – attacked an enormous creature unknown to the empire, a furry animal with enormous ears that had wandered, perhaps mistakenly, onto the valley floor. Ants of various species swarmed over the creature, some plunging their pincers into its legs, others discharging streams of formic acid into its eyes and blinding it, while a battalion of truncated ants charged as one, inserting their flat-fronted heads into the creature's nostrils, ears and anus. In its desperate attempt to escape, the maddened creature made a shocking error and, rather than running away from its attackers, made towards the advancing army. It could barely be seen as it writhed and reeled after a horde of starving ants blanketed its entire head and torso, thousands raising themselves on their rear legs and throwing themselves at the animal, burying their brandished claws into its flesh. Within a few minutes it was dead. The frenzied ants pulled with their pincers until the fur and flesh of the creature was consumed and there was nothing to be seen but its white, glossy bones.

The enemy stopped some 1000 antbody lengths from The Imperial Gate, a vast landscape of ants swelling and rising and falling like a huge, bizarrely-coloured, turbulent body of water. Would they, Adam and Zekiel wondered, launch an assault or lay siege to the city? Several enemy army ants were sent on what the Queen, Adam and Zekiel, watching from various shafts in her chamber, thought was a reconnaissance mission. They followed the movements of these army ants as they encircled the city, maintaining a distance of 500 antbody lengths or so between themselves and the moat, standing still or darting here and there, waving their antennae in the air or towards each other. Some of them gathered and, for brief periods of time, exchanged information by rubbing their legs together and inflating their abdomens, their antennae twitching animatedly. This exploration of the landscape between the enemy and the moat continued for a whole day.

In the middle of that night the butterflies, aphids and caterpillars that had been conscripted to help with the construction of the walls became wildly restless. Nothing Adam or Zekiel or their anthandlers did could settle the livestock. Many broke out of their pens and took sudden flight into the maze of tunnels and passageways. During an attempt to restore order, Adam was forced to hold himself against the wall of the main thoroughfare as thousands of animals heaved their way past him. Some, bewildered and violent, entered food chambers and wreaked havoc on the mountains of seeds accumulated over many years. The aphids, overwhelmed by dread and panic, made for the exit and threw themselves against the inner wall while the caterpillars made for the long-abandoned chambers where they dived into the icy water. Adam ordered his workers to chase after the butterflies that had flown into various paths in The Royal Tower and attempt to calm them. But he recoiled when he saw three of the insects attack with unprecedented savagery one of his workers-ants, beating him to death with their wings. These insects then flew out of the tower and back down into the bowels of the city, terrified and wild and distressed at one and the same time. Zekiel and Adam considered the chaos within the metropolis and the formidable gathering of the enemy without and sensed the massacre that awaited them. They returned to The Royal Chamber.

'Lean out of the shaft, Master,' Zekiel whispered, out of the Queen's hearing range. 'Feel the air.'

What, Adam wondered, was it that Zekiel had felt? He leaned out. It was almost imperceptible; but it was there – a swelling, a sense of flux trailing a threat he could not quite decipher, a heaving presence of some indefinable, intangible thing tightening his thorax and abdomen. Strange noises rattled in the dark of night. A breathlessness hung over all. Adam stared hard out of the opening; he reached out with his antennae. The tactics of the alien scouts became clear to both. Adam and Zekiel now knew what the livestock had intuitively felt. At one moment battalions of alien ants, once again according to species, broke free from their ranks and spread out in every direction. Swarms of green ants harvested dry leaves and pieces of bark, fire ants collected twigs, Argentinian and yellow ants hefted pebbles while all the other species combined to carry grains of sand, all of which were dumped, under the protection and supervision of the red and army ants, into five specific parts of the moat, creating bridges. Unless AntLand immediately responded, what had been intended as the first line of AntLand's defence would be slowly compromised. There was now no choice. AntLand had to take the initiative and attack. Adam and Zekiel alerted AyJay Heartland who had, however, already spied the enemy's tactic and made ready to go on the offensive.

Thousands of Red Mandibles, led by AyJay Heartland himself, thundered out of The Royal Tower. Adam looked on as the ChairAnt took command in the tumult with frantic movements of his antennae, directing his soldiers to climb one upon the other then over the inner wall; watched in admiration as AyJay Heartland led The Red Mandibles by example, running across the terrain between the inner and outer walls to launch a fearsome assault. Adam observed the red ants and the army ants hurriedly withdrawing, leaving unprotected those ants filling the moat and the first line of alien attack that was crossing the narrow bridges; watched with grudging admiration as AyJay had The Red Mandibles focus their attack on those few aliens that had made it over the moat, the Elder leading the fearless charge with awesome fervour. They threw themselves at the terrified enemy, each of The Red Mandibles seizing an alien and, with one fierce bite through the head, decapitating his victim. They tossed the heads over the water into the ranks of the aliens filling the moat who, panic-stricken, began to withdraw. The Mandibles separated into five columns, one for each of the bridges the aliens had constructed, then marched directly into the chaotic ranks of the fleeing enemy, making an intimidating, terror-inducing clamour by opening and crashing shut their great jaws. At a distance of some 1000 antbody lengths, the vast phalanx of aliens watched the slaughter without intervening, while at every vantage point on the tower, from every ventilation shaft, from the walkways surmounting the inner and outer walls, hundreds of thousands of AntLanders cheered on their saviours.

AyJay Heartland had The Mandibles form a circle around the retreating enemy. They began hacking their way through to the centre. And by early that afternoon, the carnage came to an end. The terrain between the outer wall and the moat and between the moat and the watching enemy was littered with the dead. Prior to withdrawing, AyJay Heartland and the Mandibles went from corpse to corpse, mutilating each one in turn. They returned to a heroes' welcome. A triumphant AyJay Heartland took the salute from the inner wall when the army marched back into the city. Adam, however, wondered why it was that the enemy had sent emaciated worker ants to do the work of soldiers, and why they had not sent in reinforcements from their enormous reserves.

AyJay Heartland immediately summoned AntLand's subjects. Those who were first to arrive gathered in the terrain between the walls and on the walkways. Those unable to assemble outside were instructed to form ranks in the city's main paths, as close as possible to The Imperial Gate, so as to receive his address when it was conveyed pheromone to pheromone.

Adam was the first to see the new and terrible danger. What he had feared quickly came to pass: the alien's first attack had been a suicide mission, designed to reveal

AntLand's weaknesses and strengths. The wild celebration of victory came to a sudden end almost the moment it had begun. It was as if the enemy had waited for AyJay to call for this gathering. The moment AyJay Heartland started to speak, hundreds of thousands of fire ants made for the moat, dividing into groups to form huge balls which, acting as one, were guided into the moat to act as ferries and ant-rafts. In the distance a huge column of ants formed and started to approach, numbering many millions.

The entire AntLand population of workers, farmers and nurserymaids took up position on the inner wall's walkways and the main thoroughfares of the city and The Royal Tower. The Red Mandibles and the Imperial Runners assembled on the walkway of the outer wall and in the terrain between the two walls, preparing themselves for foot-to-foot, mandible-to-mandible combat. They watched as the vast column of aliens, 200 antbody lengths wide and tens of thousands of antbody lengths long, approached their newly-built rafts and ferries. The enemy maintained their ordered, serried rows, making a terrific noise, beating one mandible against the other and stamping their six feet in a frightening military rhythm.

AntLanders shuddered at the sight of this enormous column but nonetheless took comfort in the time they knew it would take the enemy to be ferried over the moat and attempt a crossing of the first terrain, all executed in vulnerable range of the Mandibles and the Runners. Adam, however, wondered whether it might be another ruse. And that was when he knew they were doomed: another species, comprising a massive throng of raging black and red longmandibled aliens, appeared from behind and from within the ranks of this column and began throwing themselves into the moat. It was an immense rush, a vast, suicidal downpour designed to create one enormous bridge out of the bodies of the martyrs. They were coming in their thousands, hurling themselves onto the bodies of those comrades who had died before them, a cascade of the heroic against whom Adam knew his civilisation, grown soft with wealth, could not hope to compete.

The ants in the huge column, who seemed to be waiting their turn to board one of the ant-crafts, broke suddenly into several smaller columns, passed over the bridges created by the dead and, bursting ranks, ran across the terrain between the moat and the outer wall. The Mandibles and the Runners on the walkway flung thousands of pebbles onto the enemy, who retreated back to the moat. Tens of thousands of aliens, linking feet, antennae and mandibles then clung tightly to each other, forming a dense tube-like mass, thick with many bodies. It crawled like some strange cylindrical beast towards the outer wall, the raining pebbles killing some but unable to prevent its progress.

Adam, watching in despair from the tower, saw this ant-tunnel lock onto a corner of the outer wall, from where the enemy began mining operations. Once the aliens started their digging and demolishing, thousands of others joined them, lengthening the tube to the moat itself, far from the missiles the Mandibles and the Runners threw at them. With millions of aliens urging them on with their battle cries and their furious opening and closing of mandibles and claws and the synchronised beating of hundreds of thousands of legs upon thoraxes and abdomens, the miner-ants within the tube continued their inspired assault, hurling on either side of them great portions of the wall, the ant-tunnel a living, throbbing, battering ram.

The entire corner of the wall began to sag. Moments later, a section of the wall toppled over. The miner-ants' suicidal mission was a success. The outer wall had been breached.

By this time a large area of the moat had been completely filled with the dead. Aliens, with the maddened look of the starving in their eyes, ran with ease over the bodies, into the tunnel and through the breach, pouring into that path between the outer and inner walls in numbers vastly superior to the empire's soldiers. Wave after formidable wave of ants advanced at the double, charging fearlessly at The Red Mandibles and the Imperial Runners who panicked beneath this sudden onslaught. The aliens, attacking in dense battalions, successfully hacked their way through the terrain, wreaking havoc in the ranks of the empire's defence.

Adam watched from the shaft as they began to scale the inner wall, the aliens forming scaffolds with their bodies. He saw AyJay Heartland once again lead by example, injecting acid into every alien he could take hold of supporting the scaffold, using his head and jaws to knock down the enemy then, holding them down with his feet, decapitating them. No sooner was one scaffold destroyed, however, than another ten were raised. Thousands of aliens scaled unopposed the outer wall, clambering over each other's bodies, their mandibles and their jaws clicking together in fierce battle cries. He watched in awe as AyJay Heartland fearlessly threw himself at one of the larger ladders. The enemy, collapsing to the ground, swarmed all over him. Within moments, AyJay Heartland was dead.

Adam, seeing the effect of his demise on The Red Mandibles and the Imperial Runners, knew that the tower and the Queen herself were now at immediate risk.

'Zekiel, all is gone!'

'Master, our Queen! She must survive!'

Chapter 21

Resurrection

With no warning, they felt the tower begin to tilt. The Queen, Zekiel and Adam rushed to the ventilation shaft and saw a huge surge of thick, brownish water pour out of The Imperial Gate, a gigantic muddy wave that swept up the sides of the inner wall. The source of this turbid surge was, Adam and Zekiel knew, the snow melting on the summit of The Sacred Circle of Cliffs. He recalled the waterlogged lower depths of the metropolis he had accidentally wandered into not long before the Queen gave her speech so many months ago; remembered, too, the stream that had gushed past him at the base of The Sacred Circle of Cliffs only to disappear into a chasm, and how he had wondered at that time whether there was a great lake beneath the surface of The Eternal Valley. And here it now was, flowing through tunnel after tunnel, percolating into every room and chamber of the city, wreaking havoc in the empire.

The pressure behind the wave saw it surmounting this defensive wall, engulfing AntLanders and aliens alike fighting on the first of the two walkways. The powerful outpouring of water, sludge and toxic fumes, arising from great depth, brought with it all the AntLanders who had taken up defensive positions within the metropolis. They were either drowned or dashed to their death. Carcasses of aphids and caterpillars and vast supplies of seeds and fungi burst out of the city with masses of noxious clouds, creating a violent, swirling eruption of poisonous, icy water that encircled the tower, which was now creaking and swaying and trembling on its weakened foundations.

The three watched speechless as enormous volumes continued to gush out of the city with such force that murky waves pummelled thousands of ants to their death, the mountainous waves rising higher and higher until nothing could be seen of either the inner or outer walls. The body of water rushed outward in every direction, taking with it millions of bodies and mountains of rubble from both collapsed walls, a violent flow that made its inexorable way towards The Sacred Circle of Cliffs. The Eternal Valley was being inundated as they watched, converted into a vast lake awash with the dead and the dreams of a civilisation, while the tower, half of which was submerged, continued shifting on its foundations.

'We have protected you for this moment,' cried the Queen. 'Go, Elder Adam, to the viewing platform. Everything will become clear. Zekiel! Safeguard Adam.'

'But Your Majesty,' said Zekiel, 'Adam must stay to protect you so that ——'

In the passageway they heard ascending footsteps. A huge red ant, armed with a large head, highly developed muscles and powerful mandibles, was leading a team of aliens to The Royal Chamber. The Queen turned to Adam. 'Remember your oath, Adam Ant. Go! Now! To the viewing platform. Zekiel, stay and die with me.'

'Zekiel!' cried Adam. 'My Queen! No!'

The Queen and Zekiel threw themselves at the assailants. Zekiel lifted over his head one ant five times his size while the Queen sunk her mandibles into his neck, after which they used the dead ant as a battering ram, driving back down the passage several aliens. They used their mandibles to bite off the heads of two of the aliens who had fallen to the ground, hurling their corpses at teams of enemy reinforcements. The Queen and Zekiel then exuded a repellent pheromone from glands in their abdomen. They lashed out with each of their six legs in a frenzied attack then, on the Queen's initiative, looked up to farewell Adam prior to touching antennae, curving their abdomens, flexing their muscles at one and the same time then bursting their outer covering. The Queen and Zekiel died spraying all the aliens with a toxic chemical, the deadly poison momentarily paralysing the enemy before inducing violent convulsions.

Adam made his way to the top of the swaying tower. On the platform, looking over the scene of devastation, was the Princess. The moment she saw Adam she released pheromones so that Adam knew at last why Zekiel had been assigned to him as a bodyguard, why the Queen and Zekiel had sacrificed themselves so that he could survive and why he had been prevented from fighting the enemy. He clasped his legs around her body and inseminated her, after which the Princess shook him loose, opened her wings and took to the air, with Adam's sperm deposited into an organ in her abdomen.

Adam stood on the platform and watched as the Princess made her initial flight. He felt his exoskeleton weaken and his limbs loosen. He saw in his imagination her discovering that which he and Zekiel had been unable to find: the site of the new colony somewhere over the other side of The Sacred Circle of Cliffs. And when he did begin his fall to earth at last, he did so with the tower itself, that edifice tilting then freefalling, section after section deforming then sagging, the entire structure buckling then collapsing. Adam felt himself dissolve in flight, while in the distance a lone ant, imbued with his dream, would fly out of The Eternal Valley and alight upon a corner of The New World where his and her offspring could begin life anew. She would have to cope alone for many days but, in time, their first-born would mature and, knowing what he knew, do things as they had never been done by any ant before.

Huge clouds of dust and massive piles of debris, fragments of rubble and geysers of water were hurled into the air when the tower crashed to the ground, sinking quickly into the water.

By the time Adam fell to earth, there was no earth, merely a vast, bubbling expanse of water. He floated for a short while, enough time to see the new Queen, in his mind's eye, detaching her wings after alighting on a protected site. He saw the eggs she would immediately lay and how each ant born into this new colony would be fertilised from the sperm cells he had passed onto her. They would carry his dreams. And they would come to know, as he had come to know, that One, and no other figure, is the answer to all sums.

It was, to the day, 400 months since the founding of AntLand.

We are as gods, and have to get good at it.

STEWART BRAND

www.ingramcontent.com/pod-product-compliance
Lightning Source LLC
Chambersburg PA
CBHW030623120726
47904CB00006B/2017